## He followed  sweet time.

Cheryl felt as though she was in the presence of some large predator who watched her every move. She closed the door to little Vettor's room, tense with expectation. By now Marco was standing so close behind her she could almost feel his soft, warm breath on her neck. She hesitated, alight with nerves. They were both waiting for something to happen. Compelled to turn and look at him, Cheryl had to lower her head the instant their eyes met. His expression was too intense. The only way she could cope with those burning blue eyes was to look up at him from beneath her lashes.

'I'm only trying to be helpful, Marco.'

He smiled.

'Oh, I'm sure you're going to be invaluable...'

**Christina Hollis** was born in Somerset, and now lives in the idyllic Wye Valley. She was born reading, and her childhood dream was to become a writer. This was realised when she became a successful journalist and lecturer in organic horticulture. Then she gave it all up to become a full-time mother of two, and to run half an acre of productive country garden. Writing Mills & Boon® romances is another ambition realised. It fills most of her time between complicated rural school runs. The rest of her life is divided between garden and kitchen, either growing fruit and vegetables or cooking with them. Her daughter's cat always closely supervises everything she does around the home, from typing to picking strawberries!

**Recent titles by the same author:**

HER RUTHLESS ITALIAN BOSS
ONE NIGHT IN HIS BED
COUNT GIOVANNI'S VIRGIN
THE ITALIAN BILLIONAIRE'S VIRGIN

# THE RUTHLESS ITALIAN'S INEXPERIENCED WIFE

BY
CHRISTINA HOLLIS

MILLS & BOON®
*Pure reading pleasure*™

All the characters in this book have no existence outside the imagination of the author, and have no relation whatsoever to anyone bearing the same name or names. They are not even distantly inspired by any individual known or unknown to the author, and all the incidents are pure invention.

First published in Great Britain 2008
Harlequin Mills & Boon Limited,
Eton House, 18-24 Paradise Road, Richmond, Surrey TW9 1SR

© Christina Hollis 2008

ISBN: 978 0 263 86486 1

Set in Times Roman 10½ on 12¾ pt
01-1208-47017

Printed and bound in Spain
by Litografia Rosés, S.A., Barcelona

# THE RUTHLESS ITALIAN'S INEXPERIENCED WIFE

# CHAPTER ONE

WAS that something burning? Cheryl jumped from her chair and started searching the bedroom. Within seconds she discovered where the smell was coming from. The light glowing on Vettor's bedside table was covered in a thin layer of dust. She wiped it clean with a dry paper towel, fooling herself that everything was all right again.

Here she was, alone in a foreign country—no, it was worse than that. She was marooned in a creepy old villa with only a sick toddler for company. Leaning over the bed, she sponged his hot face with cool water. The poor little boy had to be kept calm. She didn't want to frighten him with her own worries.

Her fingers dug into the flannel as she remembered how helpless she had felt when RTN had broadcast warnings of a ferocious storm heading for Florence. The day staff had already left for their homes. The only worker living permanently at the Villa Monteolio was the caretaker. Cheryl had felt safe with him and his wife so close at hand. But then the storm had attacked, and when his wife had been struck by a tile, blown from the roof, the caretaker had rushed her to hospital.

Cheryl was now totally alone. She made another

quick check of the sickroom. Expecting the power to go off at any second, she wanted to make sure she could find her way around in darkness if the worst happened. This summer storm had been screaming violently all evening. The electricity had been dipping in and out for hours. *Any ancient country house was bound to suffer from power cuts*, Cheryl told herself. *If only this old place wasn't quite so Gothic...*

She looked up at the nearest carving. A stone angel perched on a ledge, holding a shield. It gazed across to the opposite wall, where a once identical partner crouched. The other angel's head had been knocked straight off its shoulders—recently, she guessed. The exposed stone was pale, and still crumbling. Now and then a scatter of loosened grit rattled down against the flagstones.

Cheryl thought of the nervous warnings the villa's staff had given her that morning. *'Don't upset Signor Rossi whatever you do,'* they muttered. *'He's a demon in disguise.'* Cheryl, thinking they were teasing, had laughed at the time.

She wasn't laughing now.

Another icy blast slammed against the northeastern corner of the house. All the shutters and doors creaked in a diabolical chorus. Wind streamed through them, finding every crack and crevice in the Villa Monteolio. The power dipped again. Shadows engulfed the stone angels.

Cheryl gripped the nearest solid thing. It was the arm of the chair she intended sleeping in, though the idea of getting any rest on her first night in a place like the Villa Monteolio during this hellish storm was beyond a joke. As she held on tight, the chair seemed to tremble. She gasped. Did they have earthquakes in Italy? She didn't know. They were on the ground floor of the house, and, glancing around quickly, she reassured herself everything looked built to last. Perhaps she ought to check the room above, and make sure nothing was likely to come crashing through the ceiling onto Vettor's bed.

Life had taught Cheryl to prepare for the worst and deal with it, but her little charge might wake while she was gone. What would happen if there was a power cut at the same time? She couldn't bear to think of Vettor opening his eyes in darkness. That was why she'd hunted out the old emergency lamp and set it up beside his bed without thinking to clean it first. It was why she kept this vigil. She was sure the power would go down as soon as she left the room. She dithered. If Vettor woke, surely the battery light would be enough to keep him company until she got back? If she went at all…

Cheryl fretted over what to do. Breathless seconds passed as she waited to see if an earthquake really would join all her other problems. Luckily, after that first shiver, the chair didn't move again. That *might* mean she only had Vettor and the storm to worry about.

After an eternity, she risked sinking onto the chair's seat. It felt stable enough, but she couldn't help wondering what the next panic would be. Outside, tiles had been falling like autumn leaves all evening. When interviewing her for this new job, Signor Rossi's human resources manager had told Cheryl to expect chaos. The old place was a wreck. So she'd known the Villa Monteolio was a work in progress, but the holes in its roof had still come as a shock.

Rain must be gushing in everywhere by now. Cheryl

glanced around nervously. How long before the upstairs ceilings started to bulge? She *really* ought to go and check on everything. Finding out what was going on would be better than sitting here worrying. On the other hand, if she went to investigate, what could she do? Water and mess might be ruining the top floors, but no workman would struggle all the way out here in this weather. Cheryl decided to stay put and keep the little boy company. Any damage to the villa would have to wait. It wasn't her problem anyway—she already had enough of her own.

Work was Cheryl's refuge from pain. Taking this job in Italy was supposed to help her forget what a mess her life had become. Her parents couldn't resist forcing her most recent disaster down her throat at every opportunity, so she'd left England to make a fresh start. The past could really hurt her, but now reality was attacking her on every side as well. It was horrible.

A tremendous squealing crash echoed in from outside, catapulting Cheryl out of her seat. The electric lightbulb dimmed and went out. It hardly mattered. Flickering flashes of blue-white light flooded the room, bursting through the window shutters. Cheryl dashed over to them and peered between their slats, squinting against the glare. The gale had torn up one of the great trees lining the Villa Monteolio's rutted drive. Its branches were bouncing on a power line, and sparks arced into the darkness, lighting up the driving rain.

She grabbed her phone. When the caretaker and his wife had been forced to leave, Cheryl had asked them for a telephone directory and programmed in every emergency number she could find, just in case. *Good job I did*, she thought, though it still took what seemed like for ever to get through to the electricity company. Half the area was in trouble tonight. The call operator promised to send someone out to the Villa Monteolio as soon as they could, but didn't know how long it would take.

A small voice croaked from the other side of the room.

Dropping her phone, Cheryl ran straight over to the bed.

'Vettor, it's me—Cheryl. You remember? Your new nanny?'

The three-year-old's eyes glittered with fever.

Cheryl peeled the compress off his forehead, freshening it in a bowl of water before she spoke again.

'I'm here, Vettor. We're at your uncle Marco's house. I've been trying to get hold of him, so he can come and see you,' she said brightly, silently thinking of all the unanswered messages she had left with his uncle's secretary.

There was no reply from her patient. Taking a fresh glass of cold water and the wet flannel back to his bedside, she wiped his face and hands, then gave him a drink.

'He'll be busy.' the little boy said sadly. 'He's always busy.'

The words came straight from his heart. They saddened Cheryl so much she couldn't look at him.

'Signor Rossi is a very hard-working man.' Cheryl stopped herself using the most obvious word, *workaholic*.

She sighed, thinking of the procession of personal assistants she had dealt with since answering that advert in *The Lady*. Half a dozen different professionals had interviewed her, but never the man himself. They were equally polished, but every one of them was doing a job, not living a life. What sort of man took on a nanny for his orphaned nephew without checking her out for himself? A man who could ignore all Cheryl's most urgent calls today, that was who. Someone whose staff had told her they were afraid of him.

She tugged at Vettor's bedsheet again, smoothing it over his restless little body. 'At midnight, the radio said all the roads for miles around were closed. It's because of this bad weather. Your uncle must be held up somewhere.'

Luckily, her little charge drifted back into feverish sleep. She did not have to dodge any more difficult questions. *All I must do is survive until someone gets here*, she told herself, jumping like a kitten as a door banged somewhere, far off.

It would be light in a few hours' time. Things would feel better in daylight. Wouldn't they?

As Cheryl tried to reassure herself, another great gust exploded against the house. Every window in the building shook. Her hand flew to her mouth, stifling a scream. Whatever happened, she mustn't scare little Vettor.

Biting the side of her thumb in terror, she braced herself for another blast. But when her next shock came, the gale wasn't responsible. A very human sound burst through the storm's racket, flinging Cheryl from her chair again. Someone was hammering at the front door.

She exhaled, feeling as though she'd been holding her breath for hours. It must be the electricians. What a relief! She was desperate to get the power back on again, for Vettor's sake. She checked her little charge and then grabbed a torch. Groping her way through the gloomy old building, she was glad to reach the great entrance hall without getting lost.

The arcing power lines bounced huge shadows crazily around the vast space. At any other time Cheryl would have been alarmed, but she was beyond that tonight. She didn't give herself time to think. Sprinting across to the imposing studded oak door, she pulled it open, sobbing with relief.

'Oh, thank God you're here!' she screamed at the large silhouette.

Then thunder crashed, right overhead. Cheryl jumped like a frog, dropped the torch—and fell straight into the stranger's arms.

He caught her, and held her close. Wind screamed around them in a fury of torn twigs and leaves, but Cheryl didn't care. Instinctively, she knew she was safe. The new arrival was sheltering her with his body, shielding her from harm. As his cheek pressed hard against the side of her head, he murmured quiet reassurance.

'Shh…*lei è sicuro con me,*' he whispered into her hair.

His voice was so reassuring all Cheryl's old fears were soothed away, along with her current terror.

But gradually fingers of reality fastened onto her again. What was she thinking? She stiffened, and tried to draw back from him.

'I'm sorry. My Italian is very basic…'

'Then I shall speak English. Is that better?'

Cheryl relaxed instantly. A voice speaking her own language was exactly what she wanted to hear so far from home.

'It's more than better, it's wonderful!' she said with real feeling. She'd been in Italy for less than a day, but her head was already throbbing. Trying to memorise new words while leafing through a phrasebook was hard enough at the best of times, but Cheryl had also been busy meeting new workmates—familiarising herself with a different workplace and dealing with a case of scarlet fever at the same time.

'Oh…I'm so sorry for that outburst, *signor*…you must think I'm a complete idiot. The boss here wanted to employ an English person, and as everyone else is apparently scared to death of him…'

The dark outline of the stranger's head dipped, and she heard a soft sound that might have been laughter.

'Don't worry. There's no need to apologise. This is the worst storm I've ever seen.' His voice bubbled with amusement. 'Isn't there a caretaker on duty?'

'He's had to go to hospital—' Cheryl began, but the wind swirled around them again. She shivered instinctively, sensing a hint of autumn in the air.

Instead of letting her go, the stranger tightened his grip. His bulky shape was an irresistible force, hustling her backwards into the building. She was more than willing to let him direct her into the darkened hall. As long as she didn't have to go on facing this storm on her own in this echoing old barn of a house she could stifle her usual feelings of panic in the presence of such overpowering masculinity.

There was a crash as the front door slammed shut. Her rescuer was still holding her securely against his powerful body, so Cheryl barely flinched. With the sounds of wind and torrents of water muffled, rational thought became easier for her. She supposed he must have kicked the door shut. She couldn't be certain, because she couldn't see past him. His vice-like hands were holding her so tightly she could barely move of her own accord. He was drenched, and dripping with rain, but Cheryl hung on. It was madness, but she couldn't let go. She was in the grip of a man and she didn't care. This *must* be a once in a lifetime storm.

Her legs gave way with the relief of it all, but the stranger held her up. Changing his hold to encircle her with only one of his strong arms, he supported her weight. Hugging her to his body, he comforted her with a voice that was lyrical, with a low, slow accent.

'There, there…it's all right now…'

Turning her in towards his body, he started patting her back softly.

Cheryl trembled with fear, but it wasn't only the storm terrifying her. Memories from the past, of Nick, came flooding back. Her mind did its best. It tried to keep her safe, telling her to make a stand and push this stranger off. But she was frozen to the spot.

Suddenly, thunder broke overhead again. Cheryl screamed, and the man's hand went straight to the back of her head. He pulled her face in tight against his chest, murmuring soft words still deeper into her ear. Now he was running one hand up and down the length of her back, his fingertips warm and persuasive through the thin cotton of her shirt. He smelled of damp linen and woodland, spiced with a tang she couldn't identify. It was a wild fragrance, heavy with musk. She felt her body tense in response, ready for flight. Her heart and head were swimming, both in the same direction.

'Shh…it's all right. I'm here now.'

Words rolled from him like velvet, but instinct still

told Cheryl to pull away. She started fluttering like a butterfly in a spider's web.

'No—I can't! Let me go... Now you're here I must get back to my little boy—' She stopped. Instantly the silent strength of this man told her that from now on *he* would be giving the instructions.

'*I'm* here,' he repeated slowly. There was real effort behind his words, as though he was working to keep his voice emotionless. 'Don't tell me I'm too late? The weather has been so bad—there are electric cables down everywhere. My car was stuck in a traffic jam. So many roads are blocked I had to abandon it and come across country. A local farmer gave me a lift for part of the way, but the crossroads below this estate is flooded. I had to climb over the wall and walk from there.'

'In this weather?' Cheryl jerked back in order to look up into his face. 'But the nearest road must be a mile away!'

Lightning ricocheted through a window, throwing his strong features into sharp relief. For a second a flash of white teeth flickered in the darkness of his smile. Cheryl saw he relished a challenge.

'I took a short cut through the woods.'

*That must be why he smells of pine needles and honeysuckle*, Cheryl thought. At any other time, in any other place, she might have savoured the fragrance, where it lingered on the big strong workman, holding her like this. But she could not trust herself.

'When you *knew* we'd already lost one tree in this hurricane? You must be mad! It's a wonder you weren't killed!' she burst out, more in fear than anger.

Her rescuer pulled a torch from his pocket. In its

sudden glare she saw him shoot her a strange look. Now she could see him better, it wasn't only the quizzical look in his clear blue eyes that set Cheryl wondering. This man seemed strangely familiar.

'The pines were rattling, for sure.' He sounded thoughtful. 'But it didn't matter to me at the time. I had to get here. There was no alternative.'

Cheryl returned his look with interest. For the life of her she could not think where she had seen that expression before. Those distinctive features and the determined jawline...

Another clap of thunder shook the building. Cheryl had been gradually releasing her hold on his jacket, but at that sound she grabbed him again.

'That one was a little farther away, I think.' A hint of amusement returned to his voice.

Cheryl shook herself, wondering why she still couldn't bear to let go of this stranger. Not only had she flung herself at him, she was almost beginning to enjoy the experience.

She pressed herself against the stranger, hardly daring to breathe. Waiting for the next lightning flash, she tried to gauge if the storm really was passing over. Rain still hurled itself against the windows, and wind shook all the doors, but the thunderclaps must have broken the storm's fever.

As she trembled against the stranger's chest, his grip loosened a little. It was then that Cheryl remembered herself. She was the only staff member in the villa. That meant she was in charge, and clambering all over an electrician was definitely not part of her brand-new job.

Pushing herself out of his arms, she bent and picked

up her own torch. Then she straightened up and looked her rescuer right in the eyes. The entrance hall was gloomy, but their hand lights and the crackling of broken power lines outside gave her enough light to make a judgement. He was tall, he was powerful, and his face was full of self-confidence. In fact, this man was ideally fitted for his role as lifesaver and genie of the power supply—except for two things.

He was dressed in a suit. It must once have been light grey and made to measure. Now it was dark with rain, and clinging as only wet linen could. And the reason he was able to keep such a firm grip on her? He was completely empty-handed.

'Where are your tools?' Cheryl began inching backwards, away from him.

He cast his torch beam around the vestibule. The action plunged his expression into shadow. Whenever sparks flared outside, it darkened still further. His frown looked threatening. She shrank again.

'I am Marco Rossi. My things have all been left behind. I've already told you that. Now, tell me, where is Vettor?'

Cheryl stared at him. *This* was Marco Rossi, her new employer? His staff had painted him as a grim ogre, but this man was gorgeous. She gulped. There must be some mistake. He'd scooped her up and comforted her like a guardian angel, not a demon. But then she thought of the time she had spent with the chef of the house. That woman was a professional to her fingertips. *She* hadn't offered any opinion on her boss, only facts. She hadn't passed on idle gossip or made judgements. Apparently, Signor Rossi liked everything to run smoothly.

*He looks a pretty sleek operator*, Cheryl thought, and then brought herself up short. This one man couldn't be allowed to trample down all her defences—even if her heart shimmered at the sight of him.

It was the way he looked at her. Surely there could never be any deceit in those eyes? They were too blue, too steady and too honest. When Marco Rossi gazed at her like that, Cheryl felt like the only thing in the universe. *His* universe.

*This has to stop*, she told herself. Her training at a top-class academy for advanced childcare professionals kicked in. She must treat him as her boss at all times. All her womanly responses would have to be denied.

'I—I'm very pleased to meet you, Signor Rossi.' She started to put out her hand to shake his, then withdrew it quickly to dry her damp palm on her jeans before offering it. 'I'm Cheryl Lane—Vettor's new nanny.'

'I'm delighted to meet you at last, Cheryl. My people have given me some amazing reports of your interviews. I'm only sorry I was away in Brasília when they were conducted. The president wanted some advice.'

Cheryl didn't know what to say. Her first job had been with an English businessman. She'd thought working for an Italian property developer might be a step down from that, but Marco Rossi was no ordinary man. The advertisement she'd answered had been extremely discreet. Figures and facts, including his name, had only come out at the final stage, when his staff had been sure she was The One. Later, she'd surfed the net to discover he was one of the wealthiest men in Europe. Marco Rossi was in worldwide demand. Now she knew why. *By women as well as heads of state*, she thought feverishly. In a daze, she reached out to try to find a switch on the wall.

'Don't bother trying the lights. The electricity supply is off—this whole estate is in darkness. Take me straight to Vettor.'

After his praise Cheryl felt several inches taller, and confident in her training.

'Of course, Signor Rossi. Though I'm sure you won't object if I ask to see some identification…'

Her voice had begun briskly but soon died away. Marco Rossi raised his torch, flooding his face with light. Shadows fell back, exposing the real man. Cheryl looked up into his iron features and piercing blue eyes. At once, she knew the word *no* didn't have any meaning for him.

'Take me to him. I'm his uncle and legal guardian. That's all you need to know.' His voice crackled with latent danger.

In a flash of alarm, Cheryl remembered the hushed tones of his staff. There must be some truth in their warnings. Right now he looked ready to explode at any moment. She stared at him, transfixed, like a doe caught in headlights.

'I've been travelling non-stop for the past ten hours. My jet was diverted, and my documents are in my luggage. That's all trapped, along with my driver. He's still stuck in a huge traffic jam. I got out of my car empty-handed. So, are you going to tell me how my nephew is, or do I have to wring it from you?'

There was no trace of warm reassurance in his voice now. His Italian lilt skated over words in a way that made Cheryl's heart sink for Vettor. Marco Rossi hadn't returned any of her calls. He didn't even bother calling the poor little mite by name. And he thought she was being awkward, when she was only doing her job. *So maybe this is my chance to strike back*, she thought.

Cheryl was the perfect employee, but this was serious. She raised her eyebrows. Then she gave Marco Rossi a hard stare. This was a man, she'd discovered, who was famous for always putting his work before anything else. It was a big black mark against him in Cheryl's book—although, gazing at him now, it was difficult to remember that. As she looked him up and down, his broad, powerful body and intense stare did strange things to her. Such feelings were aroused deep within her body that Cheryl began to fidget.

This was an important moment. She knew she mustn't wreck it. It was exactly the wrong time to be reminded of the feel of his damp jacket, or the wild fragrance of him…

So she channelled all her frustration into one dark glare. Marco Rossi didn't deserve the surge of hormones that were powering through her body. She tried to convince herself of that as she took in his powerful bulk. She wasn't going to allow it to make her eyelashes flutter like some silly schoolgirl.

'If you had returned any of my telephone calls, *signor*, I could have given you an up-to-the-minute report on Vettor.'

His lids flickered.

*They're lovely eyes*, Cheryl thought, *as clear and blue as that enormous swimming pool on his terrace…*

With an exclamation of annoyance, she broke eye contact. She had to. This man was a magician! He was trying to bewitch her with his come-to-bed eyes. But

Cheryl knew exactly what men were like. She thought back to the time she'd spent with Nick Challenger. That curbed her thundering pulse. Memories of Nick could kill any feeling within her stone-dead.

There was a tense silence. Then Marco Rossi cleared his throat.

'I tried many times. I couldn't get a signal for my mobile phone. The storm must have knocked out some of the transmitters.'

She risked shooting another look at him. The watchful amusement was long gone from his expression. He was staring straight ahead, his aquiline features carved in stone. Giving him the benefit of the doubt, she softened slightly.

'OK,' she allowed, 'I'll tell you what happened from the beginning. Your nephew didn't look well when I first arrived. I took his temperature, and he was feverish. I recognised the early signs of scarlet fever straight away. A local doctor confirmed my diagnosis.'

Cheryl had been relieved when the doctor had been impressed with her. She waited for Marco Rossi to congratulate her, too. Her new employer merely looked uncomfortable. She pressed on.

'Vettor has been calling for his grandmother. He seems to be missing her badly. Might it be possible for her to visit?'

Rossi stiffened, and then turned away in the direction of Vettor's bedroom. 'Things are that bad?'

'No—no. Wait, Signor Rossi.'

Instinctively Cheryl put out her hand and caught his arm. He stopped, looking down at her fingers. She forced herself to relax, and released her hold on him.

'I'm sorry, *signor*,' Cheryl said, without knowing if she was apologising for touching her employer or surprising him. 'I didn't mean to give you the wrong impression. It's just that—your staff tell me you don't often visit the Villa Monteolio.'

'What difference does that make? They always know how to get in touch with me. I write to Vettor, and he doesn't want for anything.'

*Except physical contact*, Cheryl added silently.

'He's just a child. He's lost his parents and he needs someone to care for him. To love him.' When a child was involved, Cheryl never knew when to keep quiet. The look on his face told her she had overstepped the mark.

Marco's jaw tightened. Turning his back squarely on her, he headed off along the corridor toward Vettor's room. 'I've wasted enough time already. Let me see him.'

Cheryl bounded past her new employer. Reaching the sickroom first, she blocked its doorway. She had to draw the line somewhere, and this was it. Marco Rossi couldn't leave a child alone in this ruin for weeks on end and then burst in on him like an avenging angel. Vettor was delirious. Cheryl knew how *she* would react if she opened her eyes and saw Marco Rossi's powerful figure bending over her in the gloom, but her fantasies had to be quashed in the face of a very real danger. If Marco confronted Vettor in this mood, it would terrify him. Cheryl couldn't allow that to happen.

'Wait here. I'll see if he's—'

Marco Rossi never waited for anything. With an angry exclamation he brushed Cheryl aside and went straight in.

## CHAPTER TWO

MARCO leaned over the little figure in the bed. As she got closer, Cheryl thought she heard the murmured words, *'Eh, bimbo?'* or something like them. But when her employer realised she was at his elbow, he raised a barrier of grim silence.

Vettor stirred, muttering something in his sleep. Marco started adjusting the bedclothes. It was too much for Cheryl. She couldn't bear to think of Vettor being frightened awake. She tried to squeeze in between Marco and his nephew, hoping her friendly face would be the first thing the little boy saw when he opened his eyes. It was no good. Marco was big, and solid as a rock. Desperate to protect Vettor, Cheryl did the only thing she could. Reaching around, she grabbed her employer's hands.

The feel of them came as a shock. They were hard, and the smooth skin was stretched taut over sinew and bone. They contained such strength. Cheryl realised they could snap her like a twig. Although she quailed inside, she braced herself and held on.

'Please don't scare him, Signor Rossi!' she whispered desperately.

'I want to check his rash. The last message I got was

from my secretary. She told me you suspected a bacterial infection. His mother had meningitis at this age. She only survived because, like you, I can recognise signs.'

That stunned her.

'Oh… Then I'm sorry, Signor Rossi.'

Cheryl relaxed her grip, but did not move. They were locked together, still bending over their patient. When Marco Rossi bobbed his head slightly in acknowledgement, Cheryl felt the movement stir her own body. Her heartbeat reacted instantly, but one look at his face shook it back into line. His expression was tense and inflexible.

'If that's the case, then hearing Vettor was sick must have given you a terrible shock,' she said. 'But the moment the doctor made his official diagnosis I rang your office number to give you the news. Vettor has scarlet fever. He's being treated with antibiotics, which are already taking effect.'

'Scarlet fever sounds serious.' Marco turned his aristocratic face towards her. 'Why isn't he in hospital?'

His expression was like flint, and its effect on Cheryl was instant. He trapped her in his gaze and looked right into her soul. A warm glow began creeping up from her breasts and flushed her cheeks with colour.

'The doctor said home was the best place for him,' she said, desperately trying to keep her mind on track.

Marco Rossi might be scary, but he was gorgeous, too. It was amazing to be pressed up against him like this, with neither of them willing to give way. He sent shivers right through her.

'I can see an improvement in him already, so there's no need to move him now. Besides, where would you rather be if you weren't feeling well, Signor Rossi? In an unfamiliar hospital ward, or safe at home with someone who cares *about* you, not just *for* you? This is the best place for Vettor,' she added, half afraid her employer would wheel away with a snarl.

He didn't. Instead, he went on staring at her with those piercing blue eyes. Eventually his lips twitched into a slow, teasing smile. Then he pulled straight out of her grasp, as though all her strength was nothing. Standing up straight, he confronted her, head on.

'You English, with your manners and your stiff upper lips!' He spread his hands wide to emphasise his point. 'Let me tell you something, Cheryl—'

'My name is Miss Lane, Signor Rossi.'

He raised one eyebrow in a gesture she wasn't supposed to defy.

'And my name is Marco, Cheryl. I don't have time for airs and graces. That's why I couldn't care less if you don't like the fact I haven't been here for my nephew. Your opinion means nothing to me. But why don't you just come straight out with your complaints, instead of tossing that lovely brown mane of hair and flashing those beautiful eyes?'

Cheryl had been about to answer back, but his last words disarmed her completely. All her nervous tension about Vettor, the storm, meeting her new employer dissolved, and she giggled. Actually *giggled*! She couldn't help it. But what sort of dedicated professional did something like that? Horrified, she clapped a hand to her mouth, stifling the sound. As she stared round-eyed at Marco Rossi she could hear her whole career shattering around her, louder than the storm.

And then he smiled. It was a triumphant gesture, as though she had fulfilled all his expectations.

The effect on Cheryl was alarming. Feathers of feeling began rippling up and down her spine. She tingled in such an intimate way it scared her. To cover her confusion she started flouncing the bedclothes and bustling around her patient's bed to neaten the far side.

'I'm sorry to cut your visit short, Signor Rossi, but Vettor needs peace and quiet. I shall have to ask you to leave.' *While I've still got a sensible thought left in my head*, she thought. Marco Rossi filled her mind and distracted her body. The silent strength of his tall figure stopped her looking at him as she spoke. She couldn't trust herself not to fall into the magnetism of his eyes again.

'Of course.'

That was a surprise. She had expected an argument. Despite all her good intentions, Cheryl looked up. He nodded in agreement with her. As he did so, the light in his eyes faded. Looking down, he swore softly, as though noticing the state of his sodden clothes for the first time.

'You're right. And I shall be no good to Vettor if I catch my death of cold,' he announced. 'Did all my day staff get away safely?'

Cheryl nodded. 'They left at around 5:00 p.m. That was when the weather warnings started to get really serious.'

'I don't blame them. Storms are trapped here by that ridge of hills.' He nodded towards the far side of the building, moving restlessly inside his wet suit. 'I need to dry off and change into some clean clothes.

My staff take care of all my domestic details, but with no one else about I'll have to ask you a favour, Cheryl. I know it's not in your job description, but could you have a look around and try to find where they keep the towels?'

Cheryl blushed. This was awkward. She was only one of dozens of people who worked for Marco Rossi. She had already glimpsed a side of him the others had never even hinted at. She had been glad—far *too* glad—of his gentle reassurance when alone and scared. Flinging herself into his arms had been the most delicious, daring thing she had ever done in her life. But all that had happened before she knew who he was. Now it was a case of an employer giving his wage-slave instructions. The change was painful.

Cheryl hoped he would forget the way she had mistaken him for an electrician in the entrance hall. That had been a terrible mistake, but she'd never underestimate him again. She would make sure of that. From now on she would treat Marco Rossi with respect. There was a barrier between them for all sorts of reasons. One short tour around his estate and house had convinced Cheryl the rumours in the media were true. He really must be one of the wealthiest men in the west. Anyone who had the self-confidence to take on a wreck like the Villa Monteolio would need barrowloads of cash to back it up. *Which Marco Rossi obviously has*, she thought.

She didn't need to look at the quality of the brand-new handcrafted staircase, or the Olympic-sized pool being installed on the south terrace to know that Marco Rossi was obviously mega-rich...and right out of her league. *Thank goodness he's not really my sort*, she told herself. So why had his almost perfect features long ago burned their way into her brain? Somehow Cheryl knew that even if she never saw Marco Rossi again, his face would haunt her for the rest of her life.

Uninvited, the memory of jostling against him over Vettor's bed rose up to tease her. For a few glorious moments they had been locked together. The touch of Marco's hands was all power. She had felt them twice now. Once in gentleness, once with determination. They were so unforgettable they fired her blushes all over again. Trying to calm her emotional turmoil, Cheryl thought back to Nick Challenger. He'd been her one and only boyfriend, and the relationship had been disastrous.

As a distraction, her memory worked far too well. Her heart froze. The smile died on her lips. She shivered, hugging her arms around her body. Not that they could give her any protection against a man like Marco Rossi! Nick was only half his size, and she still carried the scars. Marco would make a much more formidable enemy. She didn't want to put him to any sort of test.

His shoulders were wide and powerful, and two metres was such an awkward height. She already had a crick in her neck from looking up to him. As for his clothes—Cheryl looked them over carefully. His suit and open necked white shirt were obviously expensive. The cut was perfect. This man didn't have any physical flaws to hide, and his tailor had concentrated on accentuating the tall masculinity of him. The materials used were the best quality linen and fine cotton, but it was all ruined now. Everything he wore was soaking wet, and dirty from his mercy dash.

Even Marco Rossi's smile isn't *quite* perfect, Cheryl

realised. It might be white, it might be tempting, but there's a tiny chip out of that front tooth, on the right…

'How long will it take for your luggage to catch up with you, Signor Rossi?' she said briskly, trying to divert her attention from his body to his situation.

'I've told you—call me Marco.'

Cheryl smiled, and then wished she hadn't. He smiled back, and the effect was electric. Luckily, another hurricane blast smashed against the house and the moment was broken. She glanced over her shoulder, terrified. Marco grimaced.

'It will take my things some time to get here, judging by this weather.'

'Then it's just as well the rest of the staff showed me around before Vettor fell ill,' Cheryl managed with a trace of her usual bright efficiency. At last there was something about this horrible day to smile about. 'As we say in England, "it's an ill wind that blows nobody any good". While you go and have a shower, *Marco*, I'll sort you out some dry things. Finding my way around by torchlight might take some time, though!'

'I'll get my clothes, if you could find where Housekeeping store my towels. And don't worry, you won't need a torch. Listen—the generators have kicked in.'

He reached across to the nearest wall switch and snapped it on. A low-wattage bulb glowed bravely in the darkness.

'Oh, that's wonderful!'

Marco gave a very Italian shrug. 'It's always a good idea to have back-up when you live in the country.'

The increased light tempted Cheryl to run an appreciative gaze over him again. She chose exactly the wrong moment to do it. Marco sensed where she was looking, and turned his head. The glint in his eyes made her glance away sharply.

'That's very efficient of you, Marco.' She tried to sound prim.

'But of course! What else would you expect from a man with my reputation? And you *can* smile when you speak to me. It's allowed!' His response was light and teasing.

Cheryl didn't know what to think. To hear his staff talk, Marco Rossi was deadly serious about everything. But from the moment he'd burst into this house she'd been swept up by a whirlwind. He'd been protective, determined, and now he was smiling at her again.

She decided not to risk returning his gaze. It brought back memories of his hands touching hers. Cheryl didn't dare let herself be carried away like that, so she made herself stick to purely practical things.

But trying to talk about one thing while her mind was on something else proved to be a *big* mistake. 'When I've found the towels, I'll take your wet clothes off you, Marco.'

Then she gasped, suddenly aware of what she had said.

'Oh, no! I didn't mean—that is, when you've taken them off, I'll— No, what I should have said was—'

A devilish look haunted Marco's face as he watched her floundering. It spurred Cheryl into ever more desperate torrents of apology. She got more and more flustered, but Marco said nothing. He didn't need to. When he'd had his fun, he stretched like a cat and smiled with equal assurance.

'*Non te la prendere*, Cheryl!' His beautiful accent caressed her into silence. 'I'd say chill out, but you look like a girl who doesn't know what that means. What a shame you didn't leave your English reserve at the airport,' he said with mocking severity. 'Life in Italy is going to be tough if you're always worrying about double meanings. As for this—' he glanced down ruefully at his ruined suit '—it's not a problem. I'll sort it out. I'd never expect you to run around after me like that. In any case, it's the middle of the night!'

To her surprise, his concern sounded genuine. There was no sarcasm in his voice at all. That confused Cheryl even more.

'You're a man who employs staff…surely you expect that sort of treatment as your right, Signor Rossi? I mean, Marco.' She corrected herself as he lowered his dark brows in warning.

'Not from you. I'm employing you as a nanny—nothing more.' He was firm, but she couldn't leave it at that.

'I have to do something—you're filthy, soaking wet, and you might have been killed coming across country as you did!'

As she gazed into the blue of Marco's eyes Cheryl's mind was filled with images of him powering through the storm. Those pictures superheated a secret place inside her. It was somewhere she had almost forgotten existed.

When he spoke, his teasing tone aroused her most primitive instincts to an even higher pitch.

'It was worth it for the reception I got when you opened the door to me.'

There was that smile again. Coupled with his low, melodious voice, it plucked at feelings Cheryl hadn't allowed herself for a very long time. It felt right, and urgent, and…

*If I don't do something fast I'm lost*, she thought desperately. Marco Rossi had a way of looking at her that made her forget time and place. Once trapped in the mystery of his eyes, surely it would only be seconds before she was yielding to the kiss to end all kisses...

'I have to keep my mind off this storm, Marco.' She gulped. 'Tell me which bathroom you'll be using. I'll bring some towels when I've discovered where they're kept.'

Dodging past him, she tried to distract her body. His voice wandered out of the sickroom and into the corridor. 'That sounds ideal. I'll use the shower in my suite.'

He followed her, but in his own sweet time. Cheryl felt as though she was in the presence of some large, predatory feline who watched her every move. She closed the door to Vettor's room, tense with expectation. Marco was standing so close behind her she could almost feel his soft, warm breath on her neck. She hesitated, alight with nerves. They were both waiting for something to happen.

Compelled to turn and look at him, Cheryl had to lower her head the instant their eyes met. His expression was too intense. The only way she could cope with those burning blue eyes was to look up at him from beneath her lashes.

'I'm only trying to be helpful, Marco.'

He smiled.

'Oh, I'm sure you're going to be invaluable...' he murmured. And her heart stood still.

# CHAPTER THREE

HORMONES surged through Marco's veins, goading him on. He looked down on Cheryl's upturned face. Her lips parted. It was an invitation he definitely didn't need, but he was a red-blooded male. One kiss from her lovely full lips would be a great reward for dropping everything and focusing totally on getting home.

Hours of travelling through foul weather had washed him up on the front steps of the Villa Monteolio in a desperate state. He needed a break—and it had come in the shape of this gorgeous girl. Sex had been the last thing on his mind at the time, but when she'd flung herself into his arms his body had recovered like lightning. Marco's mind might have been full of worry for his nephew, but physically he had warmed to Cheryl straight away.

Now he'd seen Vettor, Marco could afford to indulge himself. Desire had been rising in him since his explosive arrival. Now it was a simmering need, threatening to boil over at any moment. Whatever the circumstances, there was one part of his body that was forever ready. It throbbed with anticipation right now. He was going to enjoy this.

Although…

Alarm bells rang in his head. His newest female employee ought to be as out of bounds as all the rest of them. Marco *never* dabbled with his staff. *But then*, he reminded himself, *none of them offered such warm temptation, so obviously.* Cheryl Lane was soft as butter. The novelty of her English reserve delighted him. It was almost as much a turn-on as the questions in her eyes. All he saw there was *When? Where?* and *How are you going to take me?*

Marco recognised consent. Miss Cheryl Lane was sending out all the right signals, and there was no harm in a little flirtation. He wouldn't admit it to himself, or anyone else, but his feelings for women were often tinged with revenge. At times like this, thoughts of another English girl shouldered themselves into his mind.

Years before, Sophie had seduced him in her parents' grand villa. He was a realist. He'd already known then from experience that the sight of him stripped to the waist and working up a sweat would cast a spell over any woman with a pulse. So the fact a titled English 'princess' had made a play for him had meant nothing to Marco at first. But Sophie had turned out to be…different. She'd had brains. Her natural lust had quickly directed his feelings to her own advantage. A poor little rich girl, she'd led Marco on and then dropped him as soon as Mummy and Daddy threatened her allowance.

The whole business had been a tourniquet round Marco's heart, twisting it until he'd sworn never to leave his emotions open to attack again.

It had been a hard lesson in how manipulative people could be when it came to getting their own way. But Marco was a quick study. He had a lot more to lose than his naivety these days. He didn't do the R word—relationships. Now he was as careful with women as he was with business deals.

And he could afford to be selective. If he decided to seduce Cheryl, it would be his first taste of a woman for quite a while. As usual, he was wary. From the moment he laid hands on them, women could never quite keep the acquisitive look out of their eyes. Whether he met them in Manhattan or Melbourne, Florida or Florence, once a woman learned who he was she wanted his wallet. But there was something about Cheryl... She was definitely one of a kind. When this softly upholstered girl had greeted his arrival by throwing herself into his arms the unusual sensation of pliant, warm helplessness beneath his hands had stimulated his body straight away. Now all he had to deal with was his mind.

He wondered what it would be like to push his hands through her rich brown hair. The need to feel its smooth silkiness rippling through his fingers rose up as he cast appreciative eyes over her. That mane of hers swung like a heavy curtain each time she moved. He liked that. And leaving the sickroom to follow her out into the vestibule had been no hardship at all. Those jeans of hers were good and snug. There was just enough curve about her to make it worthwhile walking along behind.

She intrigued him, and he could hardly wait to get her in his arms again. Miss Cheryl Lane was so different from the nerveless, hard-faced celebrity women he'd left behind in the city. Perhaps it was something to do with relief, and finally getting back here to his secret retreat. If only she wasn't on his payroll...

He treated his staff so well that core members were

loyal to the point of obsession. But new arrivals like Cheryl were a different matter. They were untried and untested. If she walked, it might be straight into the offices of a tabloid newspaper. Marco usually laughed off 'kiss and tell' stories. But things were different now he had Vettor to think about.

He looked down, deep down, into Cheryl's eyes. They were dark pools of arousal. She wanted him. He wanted her. It took superhuman powers to resist brushing that soft cloud of hair back from her brow. Everything about this little beauty sang to him. It must be three months since he had bothered to take a woman to bed. That was an unheard of spell of celibacy for him. But other things had seemed more important—until now.

Here was the perfect opportunity to put that right— if he wanted. He could tell there was a conflict between her mind and her body. Despite the invitation in her eyes, her hands were clenched and her brow was troubled. To put his thoughts into action was obviously going to take some delicate persuasion. Marco felt his body kick with the idea of another challenge. He smiled.

'Don't worry, *cara*. Anything that may or may not happen from now on will be completely between ourselves…'

Bending forward, he whispered into the sweet-smelling cloud of her hair. He already knew what it was like to have his hands moving slowly over her voluptuous body, melting her. From there it was a small step to imagining her softening beneath his touch, moulding herself into his arms as she relaxed into the rising tide of desire flowing between them. His fingers would travel back to the soft luxuriance of her hair, and from there flow down across the smoothness of her cheek. His caress would glide over her skin like silk on silk…

And then a thin cry pierced the night. It was Vettor.

Marco answered immediately, breaking the spell. 'I'm coming!'

Cheryl flinched, waking from her trance.

'I'll go!' She jumped to answer the call, still worried that larger-than-life Marco might overwhelm the little boy. He was only half a stride behind her as she rushed back into the sickroom.

'It's a dream!' Cheryl whispered, putting her secret thoughts into words as she soothed Vettor.

She told herself she ought to be grateful. He was still as febrile as she was, and this interruption gave her a chance to cool down. She definitely needed it. Had she lost her mind? Marco was filling her body with sensations that threatened to sweep aside all her good sense. But he *had* to be resisted. He was her boss, and Vettor's uncle. She couldn't allow herself to be seduced, however desperate she might be for his body. And there was bound to be something in the European Working Time Directive forbidding this kind of thing!

*It's a bit late to start checking my contract now*, she thought with growing horror. This is a nightmare situation, and it's all my own fault. If only I hadn't thrown myself at Marco so recklessly in the first place!

That had been a genuine mistake, but what sort of impression had it given her new boss?

Cheryl didn't have to ask. It was obvious. She could blame the storm, or the stress of being on her own, but what she had done was wrong. This very male man had seen it as an open invitation to tempt her with his eyes, his voice and the brush of his hand in passing. She could hardly expect him to do anything else after the reception she'd given him, but he must be put right straight away.

She sponged Vettor again, and gave him a cold drink. After settling him down, she sat on the edge of the bed and stroked his face until he was deeply asleep. It took quite a while. When she got up to creep out of the room, she was amazed to see Marco was barely a handspan away from her, a lazy smile in his eyes. He had been there all the time, watching.

Everything within Cheryl wanted him to pull her into a world of shameless passion. The feeling of relief when she'd fallen into his arms on the doorstep had been indescribable. Being held in that firm grip and re-assured by his warm voice had been one moment of perfect calm in the midst of the storm. Now her body was throbbing with his presence. Strange sensations were making themselves felt, low down in her body. She had to fight the urge to brush her hand over a place that was fast filling up with liquid warmth.

The nearness of Marco reminded her of things she had wanted to experience a long time ago. But none of her dreams had come true, only nightmares. Her relationship with Nick had ended in disaster. That love rat had treated Cheryl's emotions as badly as he'd treated her body. The experience had made her retreat from life, hiding away in her work among children. It was the one place she could be sure no one would ever hurt her again. Now this pirate of a man, Marco Rossi, seemed to promise things she was scared to experience.

His eyes focused on her full lips, and Cheryl felt her cheeks begin to pinken. 'It looks as if you're going to be one of my most capable members of staff.' He spoke with easy charm, glancing back as he strolled towards the bedroom door.

Cheryl stared after him, finding his voice softly arousing. What did it all mean? Every word he spoke acted like an aphrodisiac on her. She had never received *any* praise from Nick. Marco's confidence in her sent Cheryl's spirits into overdrive.

Her mind and body tussled for control. She felt like kicking against every rule. Marco Rossi's warm stability and the promise of his kisses made her want to go and offer herself to him right now. But her past cast such a long shadow. She had been a total failure in her one and only relationship, and now it looked as though she had totally misread the signs. Marco didn't want to kiss her at all. If he had, he would have taken up where he'd left off, wouldn't he? Her mother must be right. Thinking about sex blinded Cheryl to common sense.

*I have had a very narrow escape*, she thought. Making a fool of herself in front of Marco would have been agony. She couldn't bear to be hurt again, so instinct quickly chained up her impulses. It nailed her feet firmly to the ground, and right now that was exactly what she needed. But still her nerves taunted her. How could she trust her reactions to him? He would be spending the rest of the night here. *Not far from Vettor's room*, she thought, putting one hand to the neck of her shirt as though it was suddenly too hot and restricting.

*Behave yourself! Girls like you never…* Her mother's voice suddenly rang through her head, leaving Cheryl to fill in the rest. It was the voice of cold, hard reality and it punctured all her dreams. As usual.

Once again Cheryl retreated into her work. There was no alternative. She knew she was brilliant at her job, and it was so much safer to stick with what she knew.

According to Nick, she was frigid. He had called her a total loser in love. It had been horrible enough to fail with a bully like him. She ought to be thanking her lucky stars Marco Rossi hadn't kissed her after all. How much worse it would be to let a gorgeous man like *him* discover how bad she was at…

Cheryl swallowed hard. She couldn't even bring herself to think the word. She would just have to put a lid on her lust. If she didn't, it was sure to lead to disaster.

Thinking back to the tour she had been given earlier in the day by his chef, Cheryl followed Marco out of the nursery suite. Only then did she remember the laundry room was in the same direction as his suite. It might have been better to give Marco a head start. But it was too late now—he must have heard her close the door. She could hardly hang around in the corridor. It would seem suspicious. Keeping her head down, and without looking in the direction he had gone, she put on her most efficient voice.

'I'll put some towels out for you in your suite… Marco.'

His name was the only informality she could manage.

'Fine.'

She expected to see him stride off. That would have given her a good excuse to hang back. She was so much shorter than him, and the distance between them would stifle her embarrassment—or so she thought. Instead, Marco waited for her to catch him up. Shortening his stride, he fell in step beside her. He was close enough for her to sense the musky, warm male smell about him. It tantalised her nostrils until she had to glance at his face. As usual he was smiling, but it was to himself now, not her.

'I never thought it would be a relief to find a woman whose eyes *don't* light up every time she says the word *Marco*!' he murmured.

'Don't worry, I'm not unique. Graduates from the academy for advanced childcare professionals I attended are trained to deal with celebrity parents at close quarters,' Cheryl replied, glad he had hit on a bland subject. 'Our illusions soon go. We stop noticing people like you as individuals. In my experience, they all treat their children the same way in any case,' she finished, managing a barb.

'Oh? And you're so much better than they are, I suppose?' he probed.

'That's why they employ top-class nannies like me, yes,' Cheryl retorted, but regretted it straight away. Marco Rossi's expression had hardened. She knew then it was a mistake to go on digging in the knife over Vettor.

Luckily, they reached the door to Marco's suite before either of them could react to her words. Cheryl stood aside. It was a good excuse for another change of tone.

'I'll go and fetch you some towels and pyjamas—'

He exploded with laughter. 'I don't need *pyjamas*! I haven't worn those since I left home as a teenager!'

'Then what—' Cheryl began, and stopped. What else would Marco Rossi wear to bed, apart from that crooked smile of his? Flustered, she looked down at the toes of her shoes and blushed.

He stopped laughing the moment she realised her mistake. 'Just towels will be fine.'

Only gentle amusement tinged his words now. It gave Cheryl the confidence to look up and carry on.

'I'll be as quick as I can, although I must look in on Vettor every few minutes. He'll be so pleased to know you're here when he wakes up properly!' she said, hoping it was true.

'When are the electricity people turning up?' Marco strolled past her into his room, already peeling off his sodden jacket.

'They wouldn't give me an exact time.'

'In that case, you concentrate on Vettor. I'll tackle the workmen when they get here.'

'But you haven't had any sleep!'

'Don't worry about that. A shower and something to eat will keep me going for a while longer.'

Cheryl gazed at him, half afraid to see how much more he might take off while she was standing on the threshold. 'I hope there's something in the kitchen for you to eat. Things went a bit haywire when the staff left, and with Vettor being ill…'

Marco nodded. 'I'm glad you were here to look after him, Cheryl. I'm grateful. Your glowing references weren't exaggerating, were they? You really are a remarkable woman.'

Cheryl took a second step back, away from him. It was another compliment. This could only mean trouble. She began to wonder if perhaps her instincts were right—that only a split second *had* separated Marco's silver tongue from feeling so sweet against her lips. The next time they were alone together her resistance might crumble altogether. She could not afford to fall under his spell again.

'That's why you pay staff like me such good rates,' she said, emphasising the social divide between them on purpose. 'People who only offer peanuts get the monkeys they deserve. And now I really must go and look for those towels.'

Her excuse was as feeble as her will-power. The only reason she had to get away was to escape the torment of his presence.

# CHAPTER FOUR

CHERYL cooled down for long enough to remember where the airing cupboards were. She half hoped time away from Marco would allow her mind to clear properly. When she was in his orbit he filled her senses and turned her to marshmallow. While he was out of sight she wouldn't have the distraction of those clean-cut features and his sinuous movements. She could concentrate and become efficient, dependable Cheryl again.

Arriving back in Marco's suite, she found it almost silent. The only sound was the faint hiss of running water, coming from his *en-suite* bathroom. What Cheryl *should* have done was march straight into his dressing room, deliver the towels and go. But Marco would be busy in the shower for as long as she could hear the water run. That reassured her, and the temptation to explore his kingdom was too great.

This master suite was one of the few completed parts of the Villa Monteolio. Marco's chef had showed her around earlier in the day. Greatly daring, Cheryl risked taking another quick look. The rooms were practically empty of furniture, but they were full of sweet fragrances. All the woodwork was freshly painted in white, and the walls had been given coats of pale, neutral colours. There were no drapes at the windows yet. Chef had told her in hushed tones that they were still being made—in Milan, of all places. A single large abstract painting hung over the reception-room fireplace. Its organic shapes in shades of copper and gold picked up the colours of the original light fittings and the hearth. It put a contemporary twist on gracious living, and Cheryl decided Marco Rossi's craftsmen and interior designers must really know what they were doing.

Still the shower powered on. She edged farther into the suite. There were built-in wardrobes along one whole wall of Marco's dressing room, and a door had been left open, giving her a glimpse into a walk-in space the size of a small bedroom. She could see designer suits in every weight from linen to wool, and dozens of shirts.

Looking nervously over her shoulder, she took a few more steps. A chest stood against the back wall of the massive cupboard. Its drawers had been pulled out from the bottom upwards in his search for clothes. They had been left open like steps, burglar fashion. Craning her neck, Cheryl could see casual tops neatly folded and laid out according to type, style and colour. It was hard not to wonder how much it had all cost. *The rich certainly are different*, she marvelled, then realised she should be making her escape.

Alert to the still crackling patter of water from the shower room, she walked over to deliver the warm towels she had brought. She would leave them just inside the door. As long as she was quick, she could be in and out without him knowing. But the moment she entered she saw his wet clothes, discarded in a heap. Her mind began to work, and those strange feelings started tormenting her again. *He* had padded through here, barefoot and naked.

Then she noticed the wetroom door. It was ajar, and she could see a mirrored wall inside. It was completely clear. There was none of the condensation that a hot shower would have caused. The idea of Marco taking a cold shower ran through her veins like mercury.

She hovered on the threshold, wondering. Did she dare to go a little bit farther into the shower room? She looked at the towels she had put down on a shelf near the door. Surely they ought to be laid over the heated towel rail beside the wetroom entrance? Then Marco would be able to dry himself with something warm the moment he came out of the shower. And if she should catch sight of him through the glass wall…well, she was only doing her job.

It was the perfect excuse. Why should her employer have to stay dripping wet all the way through to his room when she could deliver everything warm and ready, within reach? He probably wouldn't even notice her.

A final mad impulse pushed Cheryl forward. Slipping through the half-open door, she entered the bathroom's wet zone. Her heart rate increased by the second. Another metre or so and she would be able to get a glimpse around the corner, right into the shower. She knew she should stop right now, turn and run. But that would douse every hope of seeing any more of this man who so totally entranced her.

She took a deep breath—and then a silent step forward.

There she stopped, transfixed. Marco Rossi was standing in a torrent of water. He was facing away from her, and nothing could disguise the perfection of his body. He had the bronzed, muscular form of a Greek statue. She watched, spellbound. He was soaping his close-cropped head, digging all ten fingers into the lather of shampoo. Bubbles sped down over his tightly moulded muscles. His skin was the colour of milky coffee, and the contrast of white foam against it was amazing.

She couldn't take her eyes off him, especially as his hands swept down over his body, working lather all the way. The farther he went the more he bent forward, until she could see every vertebra in the curve of his back. He shone like a seal under the harsh electric light, his smooth skin perfect, and with just the right amount of body hair. Her study travelled on down his legs. Every muscle was clearly defined, the Achilles tendons strong and sharp in each narrow ankle. As she watched, he lifted one foot and used the instep to rub the calf of his other leg. It was such an everyday movement, but it stunned her with its intimacy.

He lifted his head to rinse any remaining shampoo out into the flow of water surging around him. She should have guessed what would happen next, but her mind had stopped working minutes before. Besides, she couldn't move now even if she wanted to. When he turned off the flow of water and moved to grab the hand towel hanging beside him she should have been ready to make a dash for it. Instead she froze with awe at the sight of him.

It startled her—almost as much as finding a strange woman staring at his naked body surprised Marco. He was the first to recover. Snatching up a towel, he wrapped it around his waist. It wasn't quite large enough to secure properly, so he had to keep one hand on it. Dripping with water, his hair darkened and his face alight, he began walking towards her across the wet area. Every movement showed off the perfection of his body and his total self-assurance.

He held out his hand. Lost for words, Cheryl pushed a warm bathsheet into it. Swapping it deftly for the one he was using to cover himself, Marco wrapped it tightly around his waist and tucked the corner over to hold it. He was still smiling. He flipped the smaller towel back at her. She caught it instinctively.

'I think you'll find it's still warm.' He chuckled.

Despite all her bad experiences in the past, and even though he was wearing nothing more than a towel, Cheryl still did not turn and run. A switch had been flicked somewhere deep inside her body. She was throbbing with the sort of desire she had always feared. Until now her only experience of men had been with Nick. That miserable time had not prepared her for feeling like this. It was so different from anything she had ever known before. But this was a total stranger, and he was more than half naked. She ought to be a million miles away by now, but something made her stay.

Her mind whirled with the insanity of it all, but her body knew exactly what it was doing. It took control. Pulsing with a desire it was impossible to hide, Cheryl took a step towards him. The tiled floor was wet—her shoes weren't designed for it. She slipped, but before the gasp left her lips his hands had swooped around her body, scooping her up before she could hit the ground. For a second she clung to him, torn between relief and fear. He had saved her a second time. What would be the price?

Her mouth went dry. She tried to moisten her lips with the tip of her tongue. He saw, and his mouth curved in a slow, satisfied smile.

'That's the power of positive thinking. I wanted you, and here you are. I'm a man who always gets what he wants.'

Trapped, she stared up at him, white and tense. For a second time tonight she was laying herself wide open to danger. Sounds of the storm still lashed around outside, but they were muffled here in the shower room. Cheryl and Marco stared at each other in silence. The steady drip from the spray head dropped freezing water on their confrontation.

Gradually Cheryl saw his eyes cooling as he attempted to gauge the situation. She tried her best to salvage a shred of dignity.

'I—I brought you the towels. I didn't know you'd be—' Her eyes flitted over his naked chest.

'You didn't think I'd wear my clothes in here, did you? My suit's been soaked once already today.'

He was about to laugh, but something stopped him. Every sensible thought in his head told him Cheryl must have made a genuine mistake, blundering in here. He should treat it as nothing more—turn his back on her and walk away. But common sense was one thing. Gut feeling was something else. It felt so right that she should come to him like this. Primal urges were what the Villa Monteolio was all about. Princes and aristocrats had schemed and fought to live and love in this house. He was a better man than all of them put together. Why shouldn't he taste her sweet lips?

In a single mad moment he could overwhelm her now with the feral desire that was threatening to strip off his veneer of civilisation. But the look on her face stopped him. He admired her strong, capable nature when she tended Vettor. If he laid one finger on her now she would be sure to hit right back with every ounce of it. Marco enjoyed a little play-fighting, but rape and pillage were not his style.

'I think you'd better let me go, Marco.'

Her voice was faint and unsteady. With regret, Marco set her back on her feet and loosened his grip. He did not let her go straight away, but allowed his hands to drift down over the thin cotton of her shirt. That cold shower had been no proof against the surge of excitement she kindled in him. The pressure of her body against his was arousing him all over again.

'I don't expect to be spied on in the shower,' he said, the conflict between testosterone and good manners turning his words into a growl. 'Why did you come all the way in here if it wasn't in the hope of getting a warm welcome from me?'

'I was only bringing your towels.'

She had an answer for everything, this one. Standing there pink with shame at being caught out, she reminded Marco of the robin that haunted the villa grounds. Her brown eyes were bright with intelligence, and the proud swell of her breasts dared him to try anything. Marco grinned. She didn't need to toss that glossy mane of hair so defiantly. The line had been drawn between them. At least for the moment…

'You didn't need to go to so much trouble, Cheryl. Anything's a luxury after a freezing shower!'

That took the wind out of her sails—but not for long.

'I thought it would be a little bit of comfort after your cross-country journey.'

*Just as I thought. Never at a loss.* He smiled to himself.

'Don't you think I've got enough comfort, with all this?' He indicated the luxurious *en-suite* bathroom.

She nodded, but could not move. The sight of his bronzed body, wrapped only in that white bathtowel, was trapping her. His nipples were hard dark beads, pointing proudly out of his pelt of chest hair.

In one movement he brushed past her. Flinging the wetroom door wide open, he stepped back quickly to let her through—and Cheryl was only too aware of the electric charge igniting the air between them.

She walked out and heard him padding, barefoot, into the room behind her. Her body became one quivering mass of nerves. Every centimetre of her skin came alive. She could almost feel his gaze travelling over the back of her shirt. Despite the thinness of its cotton, she suddenly felt red-hot and claustrophobic. His hands had already run over her ribcage, comforting and supporting her. How would it feel to have them peeling away her clothes, removing the restriction of the bra that was right now pressing painfully against her erect nipples? Then his hands might travel south, sliding between her jeans and—

'H-have you got everything you need?'

Desperate to block the image from her mind, she dashed over to the bench, where Marco had laid out a set of neatly folded clothes. Bending over them meant she didn't have to look at him…until the moment he strolled into her field of vision again to see what she was doing. On the way, he picked up one of the other towels she had brought. As he used it on his long powerful limbs and broad chest, he followed her nervous movements with interest.

'Thanks, but you don't need to fold that shirt so carefully. I'll take it now.'

He held out a hand to her. His pale palm was in delicious contrast to the cool gold colouring that shaded the rest of his body.

Her eyes were drawn up the length of his forearm and over a smoothly curved bicep before reaching the soft darkness of his chest hair. *You can't look at things like that!* A warning voice rang in her head, but Cheryl ignored it. *Oh, yes, I can, and I'm going to!* the rebel in her replied.

'You're making progress!' His voice was a low rumble. 'I can see your mind isn't gripped by work all the time.'

There was a wicked gleam in his eyes again. Cheryl was mortified. All her nervous fiddling with his shirt was crumpling it right out of shape. She pushed it at him without making eye contact.

'I—I must go back to check on Vettor. I'll leave you in peace to finish dressing, Marco.'

Peace was the last thing on *her* mind. Her thoughts would be completely full of him until they met again.

'Fine.' He looked her over carefully. 'But we need something to eat. You'd better meet me in the kitchens.'

He was unfolding a pair of shorts.

'Of course,' she said quickly, diving out of the room before he could take off his towel.

Cheryl checked Vettor was still asleep, and then took a quick shower in her own quarters. There was one sure way to reinforce the divide between her and the almost totally irresistible Signor Rossi, and that was her smart official uniform. Anyone with a high profile wanted their child cared for by a graduate of The Academy. It was a way of displaying their success. And if Marco was like other rich people she had worked with, he'd value his prestige more than her.

She grabbed her summer uniform, a long-sleeved, knee-length lavender dress, like a life preserver. Brushing her chestnut waves back from her face, she pinned them up as neatly as her nerves would let her. Adding her name badge completed the starchy effect. *No wolf will look at me twice while I'm dressed like this—especially with thick black tights and flat lace-up shoes*, she thought, straightening her belt.

As she went to find Marco down in the kitchens, she noticed the eastern sky was trying to lighten with the dawn. Good. That meant the official start of another working day. Combined with her crisply efficient uniform, it would keep her mind off the beguiling Signor Rossi. At least that was what she hoped.

But a terrible thought began forming in her mind. What if he expected her to make breakfast for him? This was her first trip out of England. She had absolutely no idea what Italians ate.

Cheryl was deep in thought as she walked through the villa's great dining room. Then she stopped, and sniffed. The unmistakable, irresistible aroma of frying bacon drew her in the direction of the kitchens. Outside their door was a small dark heap. As she got closer, she realised it was Marco's sodden clothing. Gathering it all up in her arms, she pushed her way through the swing doors and into the room beyond.

The kitchens at the Villa Monteolio had come as a shock to Cheryl when she was first shown around. Food was obviously more important to Marco Rossi than the exterior of his house. A warren of rooms had been reno-vated to Michelin-star standard. Every surface was smooth and shiny, every item of food catalogued and colour-coded all the way from delivery area to presen-tation table.

This morning Marco stood alone in the ordered per-fection of his kitchens. He was using a fish slice to poke the contents of an industrial-sized frying pan balanced on a gas hob. As she walked in, he did a quick double-take.

'That's quite some transformation, Cheryl—' he began. Then his face darkened as he saw what she was carrying.

'I was going to do that. Chef won't want you bringing those wet clothes through here.'

Cheryl felt deflated. 'True. I'll take them back to the laundry room. I would have made sure I came down in time to do your breakfast if I'd known what you wanted.'

'Don't worry about it. I'm employing you as Vettor's nanny, not a mind-reader.'

When she got back from dumping his things, Cheryl found Marco loading a plate with food. His rich mix of bacon, sausages, eggs and mushrooms was a very English breakfast. *I could have cooked that for him*, she thought bleakly, *although I wouldn't have guessed anyone could eat such a huge amount.* He had made far too much for one plate to hold. Putting the pan under the nearest rank of heat lamps to keep warm, he carried his meal over to the kitchen table. Then he returned to deal out a much smaller version of his own breakfast to offer her.

Cheryl couldn't hide her astonishment.

'Oh…but I never eat much at this time!'

'I can see that.' He shook the plate slightly. 'Go on— it'll do you good.'

There was no arguing with him. She took the plate, while Marco wiped a couple of splashes from the work surface and adjusted the heat lamps. He looked perfectly at home—which was another surprise.

'It's a good job you got down first, Marco. I had no idea how I was going to feed a sophisticated Italian man,' she said slowly, still watching him as she put her plate on the table and took cutlery from a drawer.

'I'm getting back to my roots.'

He balanced his fish slice on the edge of the pan, then went over to the staff section of the room. There, he picked up a big brown teapot and poured out two mugs of tea. Digging two huge teaspoons of sugar straight out of a storage jar, he dropped them into one of the cups and stirred it into a whirlpool. Cheryl dashed over to rescue the second cup of tea before he could sweeten that one, too. Opening one of the fridges, she got out some milk and added a splash to her own drink. As she passed the container across to him, she realised it was going to take an awful lot more to make her own tea drinkable. It was so strong it looked like bitter chocolate.

She sat down at the table with her mug of milk-filled tea, and watched Marco making great inroads into his packed plate.

'It seems funny the villa's kitchens have been reno-vated when the roof is still in such a terrible state,' she said, looking for any excuse to linger beside him.

'Only an English person would put the look of a house before cooking.'

Despite his words, Marco didn't sound scornful. While Cheryl wondered how to take his remark, he looked up quickly.

'Don't worry. The roof has been made weather tight from the inside. Replacement tiles are being created specially. Once they're flown in, this old place will look beautiful again within days.'

'Ah—so *that's* why you could risk having that new staircase installed!'

He took a long drink of tea, watching her over the rim of his mug. His clear blue eyes were sharp as needles. 'What do you think of it?'

'It's beautiful. I'm amazed there are still craftsmen about with so much skill.'

Her answer obviously pleased him. 'I made it myself.'

Cheryl didn't know whether or not to believe him. Marco Rossi was supposed to be impatient and short-tempered. She didn't know anything about carpentry, but the broad, smooth staircase in the main hall was a work of art. It must have taken patience and a real eye for detail.

She went back to her breakfast, and for a while they ate in silence. From her place at the table, Cheryl kept a discreet watch on him from beneath her eyelashes as she ate.

'I couldn't help noticing your suite hadn't been aired, Marco. I've moved in with Vettor for the moment, so I can be on call around the clock—'

'That's very impressive!'

'He's my responsibility, but that isn't why I mentioned it,' she said, careful to concentrate on carving neat pieces from her fried egg. 'When there wasn't any reply to my messages, your house staff assumed you wouldn't be coming back here any time soon. They didn't bother turning the heating on in your suite. Why don't you use my rooms to catch up on your sleep for a few hours? My suite is small, but it'll be much more comfortable than yours for the moment. Until the power went off, the under-floor heating was on in there, to keep it aired.'

He stopped eating. After a pause to take a long, slow draught of tea, he turned the full power of his ice-blue gaze on her. Before she could look away, he caught his lower lip between his teeth and shook his head.

'That is so tempting,' he said thoughtfully. 'But this place isn't your responsibility. It's mine. And the sooner I can get something done about that Tilia bouncing on the power lines, the better.'

'The electricity company said they were going to send someone as fast as possible. That's why I thought you were—' Cheryl stopped and blushed, remembering what had happened when she'd opened the door to him. 'Although they didn't say when it would be.'

'I'll ring them again. It will come better from someone with an understanding of technical problems.' Finishing the last mouthful of his breakfast, Marco pushed a piece of bread around his plate to mop up the last of the goodness. Cheryl didn't know anyone apart from her father who did that. All the male students at the academy used to moan about cholesterol. They'd left far more food than they'd eaten. Marco Rossi was very different from them.

*And in more ways than one*, she thought with a tingle of excitement.

'The staff say Vettor eats like a mouse. I hope I can build up his appetite to match his uncle's.'

'Don't you dare! Vettor's going to be an academic.'

Viewing his empty plate with satisfaction, Marco didn't see Cheryl's eyebrows fly up at his words.

'Using your brain doesn't need as much fuel as manual labour,' he went on brusquely, and then dropped his cutlery. After another quizzical glance at his hands, he held one out to her in a silent demand. She passed him her phone.

'Now, give me the number of the power company. I want to get my hands on that tree. If they don't know what they're doing, and I'm not there to keep an eye on them, they'll chop that beautiful creature up into useless chunks. If that happens they might as well stack it for firewood and be done with it.' His nostrils flared.

'You got here in pitch darkness!' Cheryl said incredulously. 'How do you know that tree is beautiful? You might not want it when you see it in daylight.'

'It is a Tilia.' He spread his fingers and frowned. 'Of course it's beautiful.'

His eyes were alight now, but not with the gleam he'd turned on in the shower room. It was an expression that gave Cheryl the nerve to try to keep his mind on more practical things.

'Can you be sure?' she ventured.

He nodded. 'I know about wood. I work in construction. At least I *used* to.' He frowned down at the mobile in his hands. 'That's how a poor boy from the wrong side of Florence rose from nothing and went on to employ a nanny like you for his nephew.'

Cheryl thought about the staircase out in the main hall. Marco had said he'd built it himself. Maybe he'd been telling the truth. There was no mistaking the way his face came alive with pleasure when he spoke about his speciality. That made a change. Most of the time it looked as though all his successes didn't bring him much to smile about.

'You make it sound as though you've got regrets, Marco. Why is that? You've got everything any man could want, and you must have left the donkeywork of manual labour behind a long time ago.'

Marco turned his head slowly and stared at her. There was a frankly disbelieving look in his eyes.

'Cheryl, you are the first woman who has had the sense to realise that!'

'It seems an obvious conclusion. Anyone who can afford—' She cringed at the reference to money and corrected herself. 'Anyone who is as successful as you must spend all their time in an office. My previous employer did nothing but network and attend meetings.'

'That's the complaint all my women make,' Marco said grimly. 'But I don't have space in my life for complications like them any more. You'll be safe from me, Cheryl.'

He turned that knowing smile on her again.

'For the moment I've only got room for one thing in my life, and that's work.'

*So your staff were right*, Cheryl thought bitterly. *I should have guessed. That's why this is the one and only time you've visited little Vettor since he's been here at the villa. Work absorbs your life; family gets left behind.*

'I'll make that call to the electricity company.' He stood up, concentrating on the mobile phone's display panel. Cheryl settled down to wait, expecting him to be passed from person to person as she had been. She was in for a shock. Marco had been right. They didn't mess with him. A few well-chosen words later, he handed the phone back to her with a smile.

'The workmen are on their way. I'll get ready to meet them.'

'No—you must be shattered. Vettor won't want to see you looking as tired as he feels. Why don't you go and get some sleep before he wakes up? I'll deal with the electricians, if you tell me where they should put the tree.'

He put his head on one side and regarded her. 'Have you any experience of men on overtime in bad weather, Cheryl?'

The delicious music of his accent when he spoke her name teased her even when he was trying to put her off.

'No, but—'

His eyes shadowed. Exhaustion was catching up with him, but he still smiled.

'Then you can leave everything to me. I speak workmen's language—and I don't just mean Italian.'

Still glowing from his earlier compliments, Cheryl had been ready to argue. But when he said that, she realised he was right. The last thing she wanted to do was haggle with a bunch of strange men. That was why she was a nanny—it kept her in the wings of public life, not centre stage. It was where she liked to stay. But Marco expected her to be invaluable, called her strong and capable, and she wanted to go on proving to him how good she could be.

She thought back to when simple tasks like driving or operating a DVD had been taken out of her hands, because

Nick had said she ought to leave 'complicated stuff' like that to him. Whenever he'd allowed Cheryl to visit his flat, she'd been left to clean it and do all the chores. Then she had discovered she'd been scrubbing his collars and cuffs for the benefit of another woman. The worm had turned. That day Cheryl had stood up for herself for the first time in her life and said enough, no more.

She had made a decision about what she would and wouldn't do, and she still remembered how good it had felt. Now she could get that feeling all over again. She didn't need to expose herself to an audience if she didn't want to, and Marco was giving her the perfect get-out.

'OK—if you've had more practice, it makes sense,' she said, trying to hide her relief.

'It does—and I'll be right on their backs if there's any mistake. Wood like that is a valuable commodity.'

Cheryl was amazed. Unlike other wealthy people she had worked for, Marco still seemed to have a grip on how much things cost.

'Oh… I didn't know that! Good grief—I would have asked them to tow it away as rubbish!'

'Working in the real world soon teaches you there's good money to be made from innocence.' He gave her a conspiratorial smile. 'So I'll deal with the workmen. But if you like you can come and watch how I negotiate with them. You might learn something.'

'I will.' She nodded, and he laughed.

'You sound very sure of that!'

She piled their breakfast plates up neatly, ready to carry them out to one of the dishwashers.

'I might not have known you for long, Marco, but I've seen enough to realise you mean business.'

He laughed.

'That's good. And now I think we'd better get ready to meet those electricians. If I stay in this warm kitchen for much longer, I might be tempted by that bed of yours.'

In the silence that fell between them, a gust of wind swept around outside the house. Her head jerked up, and she found herself gazing straight into Marco's eyes. Their Mediterranean blue made her feel alive in a way she had never known before. He put her on edge—so much so that when the next breeze rattled tree branches against the kitchen window she jumped guiltily.

Suddenly his hand was there, dropping over hers. He encircled her fingers lightly, holding her safe and warm while the storm struggled through its dying moments outside.

'It's OK, Cheryl. I don't think there will be any more thunder now.'

His voice was gentle and reassuring. She froze, knowing she should pull away from him, break this contact. It spoke to her deepest desires, and that meant danger. Her inner woman whispered that this was the moment. All she had to do was relax and let Marco carry her away on a cloud of pleasure. She was sure any encouragement, even the slightest movement, would do it. All the temptation was there in his eyes.

She took a deep breath. It was supposed to steady her, but instead it was suffused with the warm scent of him. Her heightened senses caught the faintest trace of something wholly masculine beneath the fresh sharp tang of shower gel. It filled her mind and body with fantasies of lying naked in the villa's lemon grove under skies as blue as his eyes…

Marco moved around the table. At no time did his hand leave hers, and as he reached her side he drew her gently to her feet. Then, with a last squeeze, he let her hand fall and touched her on the shoulder.

'Look at the time—our visitors will be here soon.' His voice was soft as thistledown, his eyes unreadable. 'I think you'd better go and fetch your coat, Cheryl. I'll meet you in the hall.'

# CHAPTER FIVE

CHERYL was on fire. That single contact with Marco's hand had been enough to send her temperature soaring. It couldn't last.

When she got back to the vestibule, the chill from the open front door struck her like ice. Marco's expression had a new tinge of winter about it, too. He was talking to a knot of workmen on the doorstep, his eyes hooded as the sound of her footsteps made him look back into the house. He held up his hand, as though he expected her to make a headlong dash down his impressive new staircase. Nothing could have been further from the truth.

She needed all her nerve to stand in front of this mob. But at least Marco was in command of them.

Cheryl came down the last few stairs, each step taking her away from the certainty of her own room towards the confusion in the hall. Her suite was empty, quiet and safe. The villa's entrance was noisy and full of movement. Every one of the workmen looked her over carefully, which made her shrink back nervously. She could almost feel the skim of their gaze.

'Cheryl? Come over here.'

Marco's voice cut through her fear. He was pointing

to a space between him and the main doors. She scuttled over to join him, glad for some protection from all the interested stares. None of the workmen would dare look at her while she was under Marco's personal protection.

'See out there—it's dawn. The electricians have made the power supply safe, so we'll go out and take a look at my prize.'

He shepherded her out of the house. Cheryl relaxed the moment she felt the wild, wet wind on her face. Standing on the deserted forecourt, she could forget about the house full of men, who she was sure must be studying her for faults. Digging her hands into the pockets of her coat, she stood beside Marco as they surveyed the fallen tree from a safe distance.

It must have been at least twenty metres high when standing, like the rest of the avenue. Now this fallen giant looked sad and dejected. Its roots had torn a great hole in the ground. It gaped like an empty socket.

'That's bad,' Marco said above the clatter of branches still rattling in the stiff breeze. 'Still, nature's loss is my gain. The nearest specimen tree nursery will be glad of the business, too. One quick phone call and this old avenue of trees will hardly look any different.'

'You can't *buy* anything of that size!' Cheryl laughed, wondering how out-of-place a sapling from the local garden centre would look transplanted between such giants. As the new girl at the Villa Monteolio, she could sympathise.

'*I* can—all it takes is money. And an army of garden staff to keep the new tree watered and secure until it is well established.'

Not for the first time Cheryl thought back to what the

Monteolio staff had said about their employer. Could anyone who would lavish so much money on a tree be called mean? Then she thought of Vettor, the poor little boy who had lost his parents and was now living in the stark and draughty Villa Monteolio. Quite clearly Marco wasn't going to take on the role of full-time father, and he cared more about his work than spending time with the little boy. If Marco put possessions before people, he must have a heart of marble.

As they watched, contractors arrived to move the great tree. Cheryl stood in silence as Marco gave instructions. Once or twice he even lent a hand. She noticed he called each workman by name. Missing nothing, she also saw the respect this earned him. Thanks to Marco, the job was completed with the maximum efficiency and minimum fuss.

Later, as the workforce got ready to leave, a large black Mercedes swept in through the gates of the Monteolio estate. It was so big and so impressive everyone except Marco stopped and stared. He was too busy pacing out the length of quality hardwood the storm had given him. When the car purred to a halt, he walked over to it. After a few words with his driver, he took a briefcase, suit carrier and leather cabin bag from the boot. As the car drove away, he smiled at Cheryl.

'Could you do me a favour? I don't want to put any of this stuff down on the wet drive, but these guys deserve a good tip. There's some money in the pocket of my suit—get it out and give it to them, would you?'

She pulled the zip of the suit carrier down far enough to see an Armani jacket inside. The same heady after-shave drifting around Marco clung to its fabric, tormenting her as she felt around inside its silk-lined pockets. When her fingers made contact with a fold of money, she pulled it out. Hesitantly, she started to peel off the top ten-euro note.

'How much shall I give them?'

'Give the whole bundle to Berni. He's the one standing right behind you. He'll share it out.'

'What—all of it? But there must be a hundred euros here, easily!'

Marco shrugged nonchalantly. 'So? Hand it over. How far would a single note go in an English pub between this lot?'

He said something in Italian to the workmen ranged around them. It went straight over Cheryl's head, but they chuckled appreciatively. She shoved the money at the men, and then shrank back towards Marco. The fact that his words mystified her didn't seem half so threatening as the workmen did. Somehow his tone always made her feel more at ease with him, not less.

'What did you say to them, Marco?' she asked, as soon as the workmen were inside their vehicles.

He made an effort to remember. 'It was just builders' talk. How cute, or what a treat. Something like that,' he said airily. 'They laughed because they're more used to tips being paid grudgingly, if at all.'

Cheryl was still uneasy. 'I wish you'd said don't spend it all at once.'

The way he'd handed out such wealth sent shivers down her spine.

'You don't like it here, do you, Cheryl?'

His sudden enquiry had a hard edge. Instead of

looking at her as he spoke, he watched the workmen's vans rattle away down the villa's overgrown drive.

Cheryl was horrified. The wind whipping her hair across her face almost took her breath away. 'I do! Whatever makes you think I don't?'

'You're uncomfortable. I can tell.'

'That isn't anything to do with the Villa Monteolio.' *Or you*, she added silently.

Marco started back towards the house. 'So neither the terrible weather nor the state of this place has put you off yet?'

'Nobody can do anything about the weather.' *Not even you*, she thought, watching his easy assurance as he strolled towards his villa. This man had the sort of self-confidence she could only dream about. 'And your staff told me you haven't owned this place for long, so that explains a lot.'

He stopped, instantly on his guard. 'What else did my people tell you about me?'

There was a pause. 'Nothing,' Cheryl lied. She knew how painful it was to be talked about behind your back.

Some of the tension left his face and he laughed. 'Let's see if you can come up with a more spontaneous reply to the next thing I'm going to put to you.'

He walked on a few steps and then looked back. His handsome face was alight, and Cheryl hesitated. While she wondered what was in store, he waited for her to question him. But she had been trained to listen to instructions, not ask for them. By the time she realised that curiosity was allowed under Marco's rules, she'd missed her chance to ask.

'I've come to a decision,' he announced, pushing

open the front door of the villa for her to go in. 'It's one you'll love, if you've got any sense. And I have a feeling you've got plenty of that, Cheryl.'

Something about the way he spoke persuaded her to believe him.

'Go on.'

'How long will it be before my nephew is well enough to travel?'

'It's difficult to say. The infection will take a while to clear, and he'll probably be listless for some time after that. Why?'

''I've got a proposition for you. Don't look like that—it won't hurt! All I need to know is whether you think he would enjoy some time by the sea?'

'I'm sure he'd enjoy it—any child would.'

'That's good. It's not natural for a child to spend his life cooped up indoors. He's got hectares here, but the seaside—children love it, don't they?'

'Yes,' Cheryl said quickly, but then frowned. 'Although with autumn around the corner you'd have to be careful he didn't catch a chill.'

'There's no chance of that where I'm taking him. And you, of course,' he added, almost as an afterthought. 'I've just bought a tropical island—miles from anywhere. I need somewhere to relax and be myself. A three-year-old will be the perfect guest. He can make sure the sea is warm enough, and explore. It'll be good for him, won't it?'

Cheryl didn't answer. The staff had warned her Vettor was a frail little boy, even when well. He didn't sound the sort to swim or go exploring.

'Do *you* think sun and fresh air will do him good, Cheryl?' he persisted.

'Yes, but—'

Marco hardly heard the doubt in her voice. He was already inside the villa. 'Then that's settled. We'll go as soon as you think he is fit enough.' His voice echoed out to her.

All Cheryl could do was agree. Marco would think it was because she knew her place. The truth was that he had stolen all her words away. The only thing going round and round in her head was the thought of him enjoying cocktails on a dusky veranda in an exotic location. The image set her senses simmering. A tropical paradise must surely be his natural habitat. And that idea completely robbed her of speech.

It didn't matter. Marco was so used to taking the initiative, he was thinking fast enough for both of them.

'Don't worry. I'll arrange everything.' He dropped his luggage on an old oak chair beside the entrance hall's great open fireplace. 'The moment the little one is well enough, I'm taking him to Orchid Isle. The only other people there will be a few of my most trusted members of staff. Don't look so shocked!' He smiled, checking in his pocket for keys before setting off towards the staircase. 'I like my privacy. That's why I keep the numbers of visitors down. Buying my own little bit of heaven makes sure the only holiday photographs in circulation are ones I approve of. If ever I *must* take a break.'

There was a strange inflection in his voice, but Cheryl hardly noticed. Her eyes were like saucers.

'You bought a whole island? Just to escape photographers?'

His smile took on a world-weary quality. 'Everyone

should have an escape route. Orchid Isle is mine. It's easy to see you've never been stalked by snappers, Cheryl!'

'Is it far away?'

'Don't worry. You won't have to walk. Although I see you've got the right footwear for it.' He looked down at her sensible working shoes and pursed his lips. 'They'll be great for the rocks, but you'll need something for dancing if I decide to throw a party.'

'How big is this island of yours?'

'It's only a couple of hundred hectares. But when I'm in the mood I sometimes fly friends in to join me.'

He had been smiling to himself, but stopped when he saw the look on her face.

'Cheryl? What's the matter?'

'Nothing… It's just a lot to take in—a tropical island full of the world's most beautiful people…'

'But in your line of work you must be used to mingling with the rich and famous.' He looked at her curiously.

'Good grief, no! I only work for them!'

His eyebrows shot up. 'I assumed your previous duties would have included taking the children to dinner with their parents and guests each night. Are you saying that wealthy people's kids aren't routinely included in their good living?'

'In my experience, people who employ nannies don't expect to be bothered by their children.'

He gave a silent whistle. 'Then you're going to have to get used to some changes, Cheryl. Everything I have will one day be my nephew's. The sooner he learns how to appreciate it, the better. I want him to eat dinner with me every night—under your supervision.'

That really appealed to Cheryl, but she was still appre-hensive. 'What about the nights when you're partying?'

'That doesn't often happen. I want Orchid Isle to be a place where I don't need to be sociable. Should I decide to fly in a few friends for drinks, I'll need you to introduce the little one and show him how to behave well in company. Don't look so nervous, Cheryl. You can see it as your chance to taste the high life.'

'Oh, that's not my sort of thing at all.' She laughed. 'Thank goodness all the attention will be on Vettor!'

Marco smiled. But the expression in his cool blue eyes was anything but humorous.

Marco Rossi soon overturned all Cheryl's ideas about him. Everything she had read or heard had convinced her his would only be a flying visit to the Villa Monteolio. She was sure he'd want to get straight back to the glitter and glamour of his career.

Instead, he made his work come to him. Builders toiled around the clock to set up an office in one of the villa's many empty rooms, and within twenty-four hours it became a nerve centre complete with personal assist-ants and grim-faced consultants. Cheryl was curious, but she kept as far away from that part of the building as she could. She couldn't think why Marco would set up business at the villa. She had heard he didn't want home life distracting him. This 'home office' brought the two sides of his life together with a vengeance.

Over the next few days, Vettor got brighter by the minute. To Cheryl's relief, Marco's chef was keen to hear her ideas for the invalid's diet, and together they thought up dishes to tempt him. It took a lot to persuade

Vettor into trying homemade chicken soup, but once over that first hurdle he couldn't get enough.

During the next weeks he even put on weight and got some colour in his cheeks.

As requested, each evening, Cheryl and Vettor joined Marco for dinner. This was the Italian way, he told her. Children must learn to be a part of the family circle. Cheryl wondered why he bothered. There wasn't much to talk about, and Marco never revealed anything about his work. With so many strangers roaming the building, Cheryl felt safer shut away in the nursery wing with Vettor when they weren't dining with Marco. Although that meant she had no one but the little boy to talk to, for hours on end.

Summer's end flared with heat. It was stifling in the nursery suite, especially when Cheryl had to close the windows against the builders' racket. Finally, one day when drilling sent shock waves through their nursery tea, it sent Cheryl over the edge. She had to go out and say something.

Marching up to Marco's office door, she knocked loudly. One of his gazelle-like personal assistants answered in a haze of overpowering perfume. Outclassed in her dowdy uniform, Cheryl took a step back. The PA smiled sweetly, and told her Marco was in his workshop.

Cheryl had no idea where that was. She had to ask directions from every member of staff she passed along the way. Finally, hot and bothered, she rounded a corner and was confronted by a very strange sight. The ancient colonnade at the back of the Villa Monteolio had been turned into an outdoor workshop. Large sheets of plywood were stacked against the shelter of the rear wall.

Cheryl had no time to wonder why such modern material would be needed in such an ancient house. She was too busy looking at Marco.

Dressed only in jeans, he was bending over a workbench. Every bit as bronzed and beautiful as she remembered, he was totally engrossed in marking up a piece of timber. She gazed at him in silent wonder. His upper body glistened as those powerful muscles glided beneath his warm skin. Cheryl's pulse ran away with her imagination. Her mind caught fire. He was wonderful, and it was all too much. Her eyes closed and an involuntary moan escaped from her lips.

'Cheryl? Are you OK?'

Dazed and confused, she opened her eyes. 'Yes! Yes, I'm fine...'

Guilt washed over her like a tidal wave. She looked down. Marco was so gorgeous, and here she was, trapped inside her working clothes and her clumpy, sensible shoes. It wasn't fair.

'I'm fine—apart from the heat. That's why I came out. I've had to shut the nursery windows. Some idiot was drilling fit to shatter our eardrums.'

Marco stuck the pencil behind his ear and picked up a saw. He was smiling. 'Are you *sure* it was an idiot?' He nodded towards the end of the colonnade. A board had been put up, and was hung with an amazing array of workman's tools. It gave off the powerful scent of newly drilled wood.

'So it was you?' Cheryl said slowly.

He dipped his head again.

'Then I'm sorry, Marco.'

'I'm sorry, too, for disturbing you, but it had to be

done. I wanted to make a place for everything as soon as I could. I get tired of driving a computer all the time.'

'And so you come out here?'

Beads of perspiration trickled over his pectorals. Cheryl watched, transfixed. They defined his muscles in a way that made her swallow hard. She tried to think of something boring.

'What would your clients think to know that?' she managed to say at last.

'They have no complaints about my work. Customer satisfaction is the only thing that matters to me.'

His expression was difficult to meet. Nervously, Cheryl touched her hair. He must have this stunning effect on every woman. Now he was turning it on her.

Rubbing a hand across his forehead, he wiped away a streak of dust before continuing. 'Chef tells me the boy is beginning to eat a more varied diet. She's got all sorts of contacts, and she's come up with these.'

He jerked a thumb towards the deep shadows at the back of his workshop. Something soft and white was spilling out of the wooden slats of a crate. Cheryl went closer. Beady black eyes blinked at her through the gloom.

'Do you think he will like them?'

'Chickens?' she said nervously.

'Don't sound so scared. They're harmless. They lay eggs.' Marco told her patiently.

'Oh, thank goodness for that!' Cheryl gasped, relieved. 'So they're not for soup?'

He shrugged. 'When they come to the end of their natural life, maybe…'

'No—stop! Let's concentrate on their eggs for now.'

Cheryl looked more carefully at what Marco was

working on. The plywood sheets were being turned into a henhouse, complete with wire-covered run.

'Why on earth are you doing this?' she marvelled.

'Weeks ago a fox killed the first chickens I brought here. I thought they would roost in trees and be safe. I was wrong,' he explained. Using a piece of glass paper he attacked a rough edge with long, steady strokes. 'I don't want the little one to be upset.'

'No—I meant why don't you pay someone to do this kind of thing for you?'

Marco's mouth became a narrow line. He bent over his work and frowned. Somehow Cheryl knew it wasn't with concentration.

'You know all about children.' There was a long pause as he walked over to fetch another one of the plywood sheets. Measuring it up, and then checking, he scored a pencil line across it with a flourish. Then he looked at her. His eyes were two vivid pools of self-justification. 'This is what *I* know.'

It came to Cheryl in a flash that she understood exactly what he meant, but he would never put it into words.

'You're too clever to restrict yourself to carpentry, Marco. I'm sure you'd make a success of anything you put your hand to. Even childcare,' she added mischievously.

Self-assurance mellowed his expression a fraction.

'It's true I've never found a job I couldn't do,' he conceded.

'I'll bet Vettor would love to watch you working out here.'

His brow creased. 'I don't know… What did you say about protecting him from chills?' As he spoke, he brushed a tiny droplet of sweat from his cheek.

'He'll be fine. I'm the one who's likely to have trouble—finding my way back from here to the nursery.'

'It's just there.' Marco pointed to the wing adjoining his workshop.

'So that's why the drilling was so loud! Did you know we were in there?'

He nodded. 'I guessed. There was a very English thud when you closed the window a while ago. An Italian would have thrown out a torrent of abuse and then slammed it.'

'Sorry, Marco. I'll get back to Vettor.' With a nod, she started back the way she had come.

'Why don't you use those French doors?' he called after her, pointing along the colonnade.

'I can't. I locked them before I left Vettor on his own.'

'That was sensible.' He looked impressed. 'But it's not a problem.'

As Cheryl wondered what he meant, Marco picked up a workman's tool bag from the floor at his feet. Dropping it on his bench, he began sorting through it. The bag was ancient, and stuffed full of all sorts of mysterious gadgets. Selecting a spool of wire, he nipped off a short length. Working it between his hands he strolled over to the locked French doors and bent over them. Within seconds there was a click. Pressing down the handle, he opened them wide for her. Cheryl heard Vettor cheer with excitement. She was horrified.

'But that's—that's…' she gasped, groping for a polite term for housebreaking. She couldn't find one.

'That's *legal*, as long as it's my own house—which this is,' Marco told her. Hands on hips, he waited for her to go inside. 'I was left to fend for myself when I was

a kid. You soon learn what to do when you're locked out
of your own lodgings.'

'Are you coming in to tea, Uncle Marco?' Vettor's
voice drifted out from inside the nursery.

Marco laughed.

At the exact moment Cheryl walked past him, he
raised a forearm and pulled it across his brow. She
caught the essence of raw male sexuality and had to
stop. It thrummed through the air, intoxicating her and
drawing her eyes to him. Their eyes locked. For seconds
on end he held her with a look so powerful Cheryl forgot
every bad memory haunting her. She was his. It was all
that mattered.

# CHAPTER SIX

'I'M TOO dirty, *bimbo*!'

His voice was rough. It was in complete contrast to the teasing seduction he used when alone with Cheryl. She was glad. Vettor should be her only concern. When Marco was around, her concentration was always divided.

'Oh, *please*!'

Vettor's plaintive cry tugged at her attention. She was used to seeing improvement in him by the day, but this burst of excitement was something else. For the first time his expression was alive.

If this was the effect Marco could have on Vettor, it ought to be encouraged.

'Why don't you come in, Marco? You could sit on this newspaper.' She grabbed her latest copy and dropped it down on one of the wicker nursery chairs.

'And wreck the only new carpet in the place?' He looked down at his dusty boots.

Cheryl's mind flashed back to Marco in the shower. Suddenly she wanted to see his slender, perfectly formed feet again.

'You could always take them off.' She paused, and swallowed hard. 'And your socks.'

'Not here,' he said, laughing. 'Not now.'

Vettor wasn't going to give up easily. 'Then I'll come out there with you. I can, can't I, Cheryl?' The little boy looked up at her anxiously. His eyes were as blue and penetrating as his uncle's, and equally hard to resist. It was no wonder she had found something so familiar about Marco on their first meeting.

'I'm better now, and I've eaten all my *torta*,' Vettor added triumphantly.

Cheryl nodded. 'I think it's a great idea, Vettor. You could do with getting some fresh air.'

For once Marco looked uneasy. He took a step back, away from them. 'I don't know about that.'

Cheryl tousled the little boy's thick thatch of brown hair. 'Why not? Unless you're keeping your work a secret from him?' she added, whispering the words over Vettor's head.

Puzzled, Marco shook his head. 'Why? Should I?'

'In case it was meant as a surprise!' Cheryl explained with a laugh. 'Go with your uncle, Vettor,' Cheryl said firmly, pushing the little boy forward. 'He's got something to show you out in his workshop. I have to clear away the tea things. Unless you'd like a cup, Marco?'

'Yes,' he said grimly as Vettor grabbed his hand. 'I have a feeling I'll need one.'

Cheryl watched the two of them walk across the quadrangle. Marco's fingers were as lifeless as sticks in Vettor's hand. The little boy was skipping along, trying to keep up with his uncle's long strides. Cheryl would have smiled if Marco's detachment weren't so sad. She wondered why he found it so hard to get down to Vettor's level. Over the past few days she had decided he didn't actually dislike his nephew. He simply didn't know how to behave with a child.

Cheryl poured out the strongest cup of tea she could make. Then she strolled out to see what was happening. Vettor was crouched beside the crate of chickens. Marco was at his workbench. He did not look happy.

'The child isn't interested in what I'm doing. All he wants to do is feed weeds to the chickens.'

'That's OK,' Cheryl said mildly. 'Here's your tea.'

Marco grabbed it like a parched man clutching at an excuse. The first mouthful made him pull a face in disgust. 'There's no sugar!'

Cheryl took the cup out of his hands and started to walk away. 'I'll go and fetch some from the kitchens.'

'*I'll* fetch the sugar. You stay here.' Marco came after her, but Cheryl played her ace.

'No—I still need to learn my way around the villa. It's good experience for me.'

'I'll never get anything done while I have to keep my eyes on the little one!'

Cheryl gave him a meaningful look, and crouched down beside Vettor.

'The quicker your uncle can finish the run he's making, the sooner those chickens can be put into it. He might even let you help, Vettor. But workshops are dangerous places, so you have to do *exactly* as you're told. Do you understand?'

The little boy nodded gravely.

'There's your problem solved, Marco. What would you like him to do?'

Cheryl tried to give them plenty of time to get to know each other, and when she got back Marco was fitting the henhouse together. He looked pleased, and she smiled with relief.

'What have you two been up to?'

'I'm finishing off,' Marco said with satisfaction.

Cheryl looked over at Vettor. He was squeezed in between the crate of chickens and the wall of the villa. One thumb was in his mouth. The fingers of his other hand stroked the downy feathers poking out from the chickens' cage.

'And what about Vettor?'

'I told him to sit down there and not move, and that's what he did.'

'Of course he did—there's no need to sound surprised. I thought you were used to instant obedience!' Cheryl joked gently.

Marco wasn't listening. Concern furrowed his brow, and his voice dropped to a whisper.

'Is he all right? I was *never* like that.'

'Vettor is a good boy.'

Marco stared at her. Then slowly the tightness around his mouth disappeared. Its corners lifted wickedly.

'Then he's nothing like I was at his age.'

'I hope that doesn't mean you'll be leading him astray!' Cheryl laughed, but then stopped abruptly. That was about as likely as Marco falling in love with her. Quickly, she turned her attention to the framework taking shape on his workbench. 'How did you learn to do all this? Did your father teach you?'

Marco shook his head. 'No. I never had one.'

*That explains a lot*, Cheryl thought. If Marco had grown up on the streets without a role model, it was no wonder he had difficulty relating to Vettor. The two of them needed time together—preferably away from home. Cheryl knew the perfect solution, but it would mean laying herself open to all sorts of danger. If she mentioned Orchid Isle again, Marco might think she was desperate for a free holiday on his tropical island. Worse, he might assume she was making a play for him.

'That's why I want my nephew to have all the advantages I never had and none of the distractions,' Marco announced suddenly. Then his voice dropped to a murmur again, so Vettor could not hear. 'I am responsible for what happened to his mother—my sister. That is why I have brought him here.'

Cheryl felt she might be getting to the heart of the problem. She waited in suspense, but Marco was concentrating on his work. Eventually, she felt bound to ask.

'What happened?'

'My sister was much younger than me—and while I was abroad working, building up this empire, she steadily went off the rails.'

Deep in concentration, Marco ran one hand along the piece of wood he was working on. Stopping suddenly, he frowned down at his finger. A splintery spike had plunged into his skin. When he pulled it out, a bead of blood sprang up. He sucked it away, and then picked up a piece of sandpaper before speaking again.

'I didn't see it happening. And by the time I found out that the money I'd sent to support her hadn't been spent on food and bills it was too late…'

He started scrubbing his work smooth with such energy that Cheryl decided not to ask any more questions. Whatever had happened between Marco and his sister put her own worries in the shade. She had to do what was best for Vettor. Both Marco and Vettor needed time away from here. Cheryl decided she must broach the subject of Marco's island in the sun. Her modesty could go to hell if it meant doing him and Vettor some good.

'Marco—if you're still keen to take Vettor to Orchid Isle, I think you should go as soon as possible. You both need a holiday, and it will give you a chance to get to know each other.'

Both Vettor and Marco stared at her. Vettor was the first to break the sultry silence.

'I don't have to go on my own, do I?'

'Your uncle Marco will be looking after you,' Cheryl said brightly, smiling at him.

Her employer did not smile back. 'Don't worry, *bimbo*. Cheryl will be there, too.'

Everything light and optimistic fled from her mind as she saw Marco's face. She wouldn't have to spend the holiday of a lifetime worrying about sending out the wrong signals. The way Marco was looking at her right now, he'd be immune to them.

'OK. You're the boss,' Cheryl said, trying not to sound too enthusiastic about the trip. Taking this job at the Villa Monteolio had been Cheryl's first taste of life away from England. To be whisked to a tropical island so soon after arriving here would be another step closer to heaven. But right now Marco didn't look as though he'd appreciate a gush of thanks, so she restricted herself to a small, tight smile.

Marco bent over his work again. She could not see his expression, and he didn't look at her as he replied.

'So that's decided. We all leave for Orchid Isle first thing in the morning.'

* * *

From that moment the atmosphere between Cheryl and Marco changed. She sensed he wanted to put some distance between them. The practical part of her mind knew this was how it should be. Yet every other piece of her ached to experience something more. Her whole body was restless for him.

She tried to divert herself by encouraging Vettor to make a little patch of garden outside the nursery wing. While he sat in the sun she worked the soil, and they made plans together. The little boy's English was improving as fast as her Italian. Marco hardly noticed. He was too busy working.

Cheryl flicked glances at him whenever she thought Vettor wasn't looking. Marco didn't notice. Feeling the sun on her back was lovely, but it was no substitute for the touch of his skin. Working the warm, promising soil could not stifle the thought of running her hands over the tightly packed bulk of Marco's muscles.

She was in such turmoil that when he finally spoke to her, she gasped.

'No need to panic—I only wanted to tell you both this henhouse is ready.'

Vettor leapt from his chair and rushed across the courtyard. 'Can I put the chickens in, Uncle Marco? You *said*!'

He reached Marco before Cheryl managed to get up from her hands and knees. Marco looked down on her in amusement as she brushed dust from her skirt.

'Looking like that, you can hardly complain if the child wants to get dirty.'

Cheryl was crushed. Of all the times to catch Marco's attention, she had to do it with grubby hands!

And then she looked into his eyes. Was that another twinkle? She blinked, and it disappeared. If it had ever been there at all. She sighed, watching him as he watched Vettor.

'Why don't you explain to Vettor how the hen-house works?' she prompted, if only to keep Marco's attention away from the dust on the front of her uniform.

He cocked his head, as though the details were obvious, but started running through them anyway.

'If your chickens aren't scratching about on the grass, they can stay nice and dry in their house. When they want to lay, they'll make a nest in one of these little boxes. Every day you can open the lid—' he demonstrated as Vettor watched, fascinated '—and collect the eggs. I'll carry it around to that patch of short grass below the terrace, then you can put the birds into their new home.'

'Can't it stay here?' Cheryl frowned. 'It would be so much better if Vettor could see the birds from his room. He could take some responsibility for them.'

Marco looked at her with quizzical amusement. 'I thought a top-class English nanny like you might be worried about germs.'

She looked up and caught his gaze, drinking in every feature of his face. She knew it so well she could have sketched him from memory, but she still wanted more. Only conscience made her tear her gaze away.

'Right now I'd rather Vettor had something to keep him occupied while he's convalescing, Marco.'

'Fine. So it will be your responsibility to make sure the staff are prepared to look after your pets while you're away, *bimbo*.'

The little boy looked from Marco to Cheryl and back again, puzzled.

Cheryl ruffled his hair affectionately. 'Remember? Your uncle is taking you to the seaside.'

'And you, too,' Marco directed at her. 'We can't possibly go without our indispensable Cheryl.'

Marco's words haunted Cheryl for the rest of the day. He'd called her *indispensable*.

She was still enjoying the memory of it when she got up at 5:00 a.m. the next morning. She indulged herself with a long, deep bath, full of bubbles. Orchid Isle was hours away, so she wanted to start the day feeling fresh. Travelling alongside Marco was bound to send her temperature soaring.

Dusting plenty of powder over her body, and adding a spritz of perfume, she dressed in a clean uniform and started work. While Vettor was eating his breakfast she filled a trunk with everything he would need for a few weeks in the sun. He might have more clothes and toys than any child she had ever cared for, but Cheryl wasn't impressed. She was worried. After watching Marco with his nephew, she guessed he gave his staff an open chequebook. Anything this child wanted, he got. That was a recipe for disaster.

Luckily, Vettor was so young he was more confused than spoiled by all the luxury. Cheryl hoped she could make Marco see that company was the real key to Vettor's heart before it was too late.

As she made arrangements for their things to be taken downstairs, the cold voice of reason tried to attract her attention. All accounts of Marco Rossi, billionaire, made him sound like a classic predator. His worldwide romances left a trail of broken hearts. *And that's only the ones the newspapers learn about,* Cheryl thought. *Who knows how many ordinary girls like me he's had?*

She nibbled her lip. *It's madness to carry on working here when I'm so tempted,* she thought. Then she looked at Vettor and smiled. This little chap couldn't be left to fend for himself. It was her duty to look after him, even though it meant being a hostage to her feelings for his uncle. She hesitated and thought about what might happen the next time her eyes met Marco's, or their hands accidentally brushed in passing….

*I'm bound to get my fingers burned,* she thought nervously. *And not only by the tropical sun.*

Staff took Cheryl and Vettor's luggage down to the entrance hall. Despite the heat, Cheryl still carried her coat over her arm. Her uniform was the one thing that could cool her thoughts about Marco. *My job is to look after Vettor,* she repeated to herself over and over again. That was the only thing guaranteed to keep her on the straight and narrow path. *And if I can persuade Marco to try entertaining his nephew, too, that will be a bonus. If only they could get on together,* she thought, remembering how uncomfortable Marco always looked when he was with Vettor.

The front doors of the villa were standing open, and Marco's voice drifted in from outside. The effect on Cheryl was electric. Her heart jumped. She picked up her bag, then put it down again. Taking Vettor by the hand, she crossed to the doorway.

Marco's shadow swept across the step. She hesitated. The sun was still low. His silhouette stretched across the forecourt, emphasising his impressive build. As she chivvied Vettor through the open door, she quailed at the thought of meeting Marco's gaze once more. His piercing blue eyes missed nothing. He was sure to know what she was thinking, and Cheryl didn't feel able to resist his scrutiny. Sure enough, when she managed to look up, Marco's eyes were running right over her.

She gripped the edge of the front door for support, and then saw his glance home in on her bleached knuckles. She dropped her hand immediately. His expression was unthreatening, but that didn't stop Cheryl being afraid. She thought back to one of Nick Challenger's favourite sayings: *knowledge is power.* She didn't want Marco to find out how nervous she was, so she turned her features into a carefully blank canvas.

'I'll start loading these cases into the car,' Marco said, after they'd exchanged a few meaningless pleasantries about the weather.

'You'll do that yourself?' She was amazed. Her previous employers had found it a strain even to speak to her, much less do anything for themselves.

Marco was already halfway across the vestibule.

'Of course.' He looked as puzzled by her question as he was by her single case. 'Where's the rest?'

Cheryl shook her head. 'This is all I've got.'

Marco looked frankly disbelieving. Cheryl hustled Vettor across the forecourt. In the past, Nick had taunted her about her appearance. She couldn't bear to think Marco was about to do the same thing. It would smash all her beautiful illusions of him.

Marco stowed her case away in the boot of the car. He was about to get into the spacious back seat when he remembered something.

'I forgot to say hello to you, little one.'

Striding back to them, he gave the little boy a formal handshake. Cheryl's heart sank. It reminded her of some grainy black and white film footage she'd once seen of a lonely, bewildered little prince being greeted like a diplomat by his returning mother, herself a queen. *If I had a nephew who was leaving the house for the first time in days I'd hug him and hug him and never let him go*, she thought.

Her mood darkened further as Marco bent to speak to the little boy.

'I'll need peace to work while we travel. And sometimes Cheryl and I will have grown-up things to discuss. So would you mind sitting in the front of the car?'

Vettor was being sidelined *already*! Cheryl erupted with anger.

'No, Marco! You can't do that to him!'

She should have saved her breath. Nobody noticed. Vettor was already launching himself into the front passenger seat, while the chauffeur and Marco were too busy laughing at his screams of delight.

'It was always my dream to ride next to a driver when I was a child. It's good to know some things don't change,' Marco told Cheryl. He stopped smiling when he saw the look on her face. 'I've had a booster seat put in place for him already. That is the law in England, isn't it?'

'Yes, but...' Cheryl began. Then she went quiet. The truth was that there could *be* no but. *She* was supposed to be the one who knew what children needed. Marco was ahead of her on points today. 'Yes, but I thought *I'd* be sitting in the front. You ought to spend more time with him, Marco, as you're away from home so much.'

Her cheeks burned. Marco had a suitably abrupt answer.

'I'm happier keeping my distance. I think he might be scared of me.'

'I wonder why?' Cheryl murmured, as Marco stuck out an arm and opened the rear door of the car for her. Every movement he made was quick. His decisions were made in a split second. Even his laughter could be threatening—a low rumble echoing up from that wide chest.

'I'm sure you'll find it all so easy when you have children of your own.' He grimaced as the chauffeur eased their car down the uneven drive of the villa.

'As a matter of fact I used to have one hundred and twenty-six children—all boys.' Cheryl smiled. 'While I was studying at the academy I did some work experience at an exclusive boys' boarding school.'

'Then you'll know they need careful handling. There's a fine line between setting reasonable guidelines and making them rebellious.'

Cheryl stared at him. It sounded uncannily as if Marco Rossi knew exactly what he was talking about.

When they got to the airport, sinister men in smart suits and dark glasses swept them past all the formalities and onto Marco's private jet.

'This is a world away from the hours I spent queuing

to get here from England,' Cheryl said as she settled Vettor at the window with a cold drink.

'I wasted too much of my life in queues when I worked in England years ago. This is the only way to travel.' Marco settled back in his seat, waiting for his laptop to be delivered to him.

'Where in England were you working?' Cheryl sat down next to Vettor. His hand luggage was full of activities and storybooks, but for the moment the little boy was happy to watch the ground crew checking around outside.

'I stayed all over the place. I found jobs wherever there was building work to be done. One week here, a month there. It's like that with casual labour.'

'You were a *builder*?' Cheryl marvelled. Looking at him now, in his beautifully cut suit and crisp white shirt, she knew Marco would never have been guilty of sagging jeans or showing off too much backside.

'You don't get to be a success in any business without starting at the bottom.'

Cheryl hiccupped with laughter at the coincidence of his words.

'What's so funny?' He looked at her quizzically.

'Nothing—I was just thinking about something, that's all.' Cheryl tore her eyes away from his, but Marco wasn't satisfied.

'Come on—share the joke.'

He looked so totally at ease, slipping off his smart jacket. Cheryl was lured into saying more than she should.

'OK—it's just that you're the last man on earth I'd expect to see leaning on a shovel, reading the tabloids or eating bacon rolls!'

His expression altered in an instant. In the time it took Cheryl to catch her breath it changed from mild amusement to dark suspicion.

'Don't forget who made a home for those chickens. Remind me to show you what else I can do some time,' he drawled.

Cheryl felt bound to respond. 'I meant that you're far too sophisticated to do a job like that.'

Marco glanced down at his work-roughened hands. She followed his gaze. His thumbs were making tiny circling movements over the tips of his fingers. She watched, entranced.

'You must be right, Cheryl. My hands agree with you, at least.'

A steward arrived with his computer. Settling it on his lap, Marco flipped open its lid. Straight away he was engrossed in his work. Cheryl's dreams shattered like the *torroncino* she scattered over Vettor's freshly made dish of vanilla ice cream.

Marco had shut her out again, and she had no idea why.

# CHAPTER SEVEN

ORCHID ISLE was a little patch of heaven in the middle of the ocean. As Marco's plane began its descent, he looked up from his work and pointed out of the window. It was almost dark, but Cheryl could still see a green oasis ringed by silver sand and creamy waves. It was beyond the wildest dreams of a girl from a poor estate.

'Give the steward your order, Cheryl.' Marco gently encouraged her away from the window. 'Then cocktails can be ready in your apartment when you get there.'

She was agog. 'I've never tasted a cocktail in my life! What are they like?'

'They can be made from fruit juice, alcohol, or any combination of the two. Ask and it's yours,' Marco replied in a voice as smooth as the azure sea beneath them. His eyes were as calm as the water, and for once Cheryl didn't feel embarrassed to find him looking at her. The mixture of excitement and adrenaline powering through her veins made her reckless. But the one thing she really desired was the single thing she could never ask for—him.

'I'll have whatever you're drinking.' she announced boldly. Marco frowned.

'OK. But I've got some things to attend to, and I normally stick to soft drinks when I'm working. Are you happy to do the same?'

'Of course. I'd never drink alcohol when I'm in charge of Vettor.'

Marco raised a brow. 'He'll be in bed by the time you taste it.'

'I don't know about that!' Cheryl pointed across the cabin to where Vettor was gazing out of a window, his face pressed against the glass. 'He's so excited I'll be lucky to get him to sleep before dawn tomorrow!'

Marco's laugh was as smooth as silk as he closed down his computer and they got ready to land. 'Well, if he's awake make sure you don't miss the sunset. The ones on Orchid Isle are unbeatable.'

Breathlessly, Cheryl waited for him to go further, daring to hope he'd say he'd join them, but he never did. Once the plane had landed he walked away, leaving Cheryl and Vettor alone on the landing strip.

Cheryl tried to be glad. She told herself it was all for the best. Sharing a tropical dusk with Marco Rossi was a temptation she really wouldn't have been able to resist.

Orchid Isle was all Cheryl's fantasies come true. It was wild and untouched, a real Garden of Eden. The only development was a small complex of buildings designed to nestle sensitively into their surroundings. There were luxury apartments for Marco and his guests, a natural pool camouflaged with ferns, mosses and orchids, and a fully stocked outdoor dining area and bar. The privileged visitors to Orchid Isle had everything they could ever need at their fingertips. Everyone blossomed from the moment they touched down.

Next morning, Vettor bounced out of his bedroom a different child. He was desperate to run and explore the beach and its wonders. Cheryl felt the pressures of her new job lift as she chased after him. Suddenly Marco's low chuckle echoed across the sand. Standing at the top of the beach, he raised his hand in a casual greeting. Stripped for swimming, he looked even taller and more impressive than usual. *Paradise really is his natural habitat*, Cheryl realised. They raced up to meet him.

'Cheryl! What on earth have you got on?' Marco looked almost bewildered. Sunlight flickered through the palm trees and glimmered over his golden skin.

'My uniform, of course. I'm on duty.'

'You don't need to bother with all that formality here.' He rolled his eyes, as if silently saying *Women!*

'No—really—I'm happier dressed like this. I keep telling you, I came here expecting to work,' Cheryl persisted.

'Oh, come on. Don't tell me you haven't got a few fancy things packed away somewhere,' he scoffed, secure in the knowledge that most women he knew always travelled with a designer wardrobe.

'It's not as though I'll be partying. Fancy clothes are the last thing on my mind.'

He stopped smiling.

'OK—so what exactly *have* you brought with you?'

'Some changes of uniform, jeans, a couple of tops—'

'No dresses? Don't you have a bikini? Or pretty shoes?'

His disbelieving expression shrank Cheryl instantly.

Her experience of socialising was limited. She rarely went to parties. Lurking in a kitchen with a lot of other singles was not her idea of a good time. Instead, she filled her days with work. Out of hours, she lived in scruffy casuals and comfortable lace-up flatties.

'I've been meaning to buy some,' she fibbed. 'It's just a case of getting to the shops.'

'That's easy enough. What do you need? I'll make a few phone calls.'

'Wait!' Cheryl put one hand to her forehead. Her mind was in a whirl. 'There aren't any shops here! It's nothing but beach and jungle. How can I possibly go off shopping?'

'I'm not asking you to go anywhere.' Marco gave her a wolfish smile. 'I want you to get some suitable clothes. And when I want something the shops come to me.'

To Cheryl's amazement, that was exactly what happened. It wasn't long before a big helicopter floated in from the mainland. While she watched from a safe distance with Vettor, dozens of interesting boxes were unloaded. Staff ferried them to her apartment. Cheryl didn't have to do a thing. She stared after them, wondering what would be inside all the mysterious packages. Then the sound of Marco softly clearing his throat brought her back—but not to reality.

'It's all yours, Cheryl. Your rooms are currently being filled with a selection of anything and everything the young nanny around Orchid Isle could possibly desire. So now it's up to you. You must choose what you'd like.'

Alarmed, Cheryl shook her head. 'I'm sorry. I can't possibly… How can I let you go to all this trouble just for me? I should have been better organised and brought more clothes. It's nobody's problem but my own.'

'Oh, but it is. This is supposed to be a relaxing break for me. Even my stewards are all in casuals,' he murmured, gesturing towards the nearest barman. He was wearing shorts and a shirt as bright as the sunlight. 'That uniform of yours is nothing but a grim reminder of working days.'

Cheryl looked down at the sand. She was hoping he would think her blush sprang from embarrassment. In reality the soft intimacy of his voice was making her flush with guilt. A torrent of wild warmth rushed through her lower body. She was thinking of those moments during the storm when he'd held her in his arms, pressing her against him and whispering his divine Italian reassurances into her ear…

'Everything is being set up for you, Cheryl. It's all ready to wear, so just decide what you'd like. Put it on one side, with a note of any alterations you'll need, and I'll settle up with the couturiers.'

That snapped Cheryl out of her dream. 'I can't possibly let you pay for me!'

'Why not?' Marco's scepticism changed to open disbelief. 'Isn't it every woman's dream come true—to take everything on offer and to hell with the cost?'

'Not *this* woman.' Cheryl underlined her statement by putting her hands firmly on her hips. 'You're right, Marco—this is like a wonderful dream come true for me. But I'd feel happier paying my way. You're already giving me this chance of a wonderful tropical holiday. It was my fault I didn't bring the right clothes. Let me make a contribution towards the cost.'

He frowned, puzzled. 'You'll be on call all day and all night, looking after my nephew. I don't call that much of a holiday.'

'I love my work—' She stopped, and pulled a wry face. 'Actually, that always seems a funny word to use—'

'You think love is a funny word?' Marco's blue eyes flashed a warning.

'No, I meant work.' Cheryl frowned at his interruption. 'I like Vettor. He's a dear little boy. Looking after him is no trouble at all. In fact…' She suddenly saw a chance for some bridge-building. 'Why don't you take charge of him for a while, Marco? I can hardly keep him with me while I'm trying on clothes, can I?'

Marco shook his head almost imperceptibly. Something in his eyes told of deep reasons why he kept his distance from the little boy.

'We are talking about your new clothes.' He recovered smoothly. Putting one hand to his chin, he stroked it thoughtfully with the same care he had used when touching her, on that first night at the Villa Monteolio. Cheryl ran the tip of her tongue over her lips. They tingled with anticipation.

'Everything will be fine, Cheryl. You can go in there on your own, lock all your doors and try on whatever you like in total privacy.'

Taking her courage in both hands, Cheryl persisted. 'While I do that, why don't you take Vettor off and show him the forest?'

The little boy had already started back towards the complex, looking for someone to serve him with ice cream.

'The staff can do that for me.' Marco turned away

from her and started to follow in his nephew's footsteps. He did not look back as he spoke.

Cheryl sighed. There was no point trying to force Marco to love Vettor. It would be easier to try to reject his offer of new clothes.

She ran to catch up with him. Marco might not be the world's best guardian, but Orchid Isle was a beautiful place. It might take time, but there was so much magic here it was bound to work on him eventually. She wouldn't give up hope yet. Especially if Marco was already keen for her to leave the formality of her uniform behind.

'How did you know what size to ask for, Marco? Have you been through my things?' she said as they walked towards the low thatched-roof buildings.

He stopped dead. His eyes flashed with such power Cheryl flinched. When he saw her reaction he bit his lip and walked on.

'Some men might get their kicks by intimidating women. I enjoy women in a different way. That's given me plenty of practice in some things, so I guessed you'd be about an English size twelve.'

Cheryl opened her eyes still wider. He was spot on! Marco was obviously an expert at this game. How many girls had been through his hands? She brought herself up short at that, but managed a smile at the double meaning. She was careful not to let him see it. What sort of special treatment had his other women received to make Marco such a very good judge of the female body? It made her wonder, and her heart galloped.

'I told them to bring everything, in all of the colours. Now, come on—you're wasting time.'

They reached her apartment. 'So, what are your first impressions of all this, Cheryl?'

'I—I don't know.'

Marco clicked his tongue. 'Oh, come on. You must have some opinion. *Dio*, you have always got plenty to say on other subjects!'

It was a good-natured rebuke, but Cheryl's mind was on something else. Tempting warmth was creeping through her body. This paradise, his generosity, the way the sunlight filtered through the leaves overhead, softening the look in his blue eyes…

'To be honest, I—I feel way out of my depth. I didn't grow up surrounded by wealth and luxury like this…'

'Then learn to enjoy it now. As a child I had nothing. A latchkey kid from the wrong side of town. I used my head and escaped. Common sense and hard work got me all this. And a nanny like you, too. Now you're here, you'd better make the most of everything I have to offer.'

For a single second their eyes met. Marco's mouth curved into a devastating smile. He took a step towards her, halving the distance between them. There could be no resisting him now. He looked down at her so knowingly that Cheryl knew her fate was sealed. Surely it was only a matter of seconds…

'This isn't a good idea…' she whispered. As the last of her self-control shredded, the fear returned. She felt the full power of him as he stared down at her…

And then he turned away.

'Decide what you want. I'll be back later to see how you're getting on.'

He walked off in the direction of the beach bar. Cheryl gazed after him. Once again her mind was on fire with thoughts of what might have been. It didn't take a genius to explain Marco's darkened eyes and shallow breathing. He was simmering with lust as much as she was. The sultry surroundings of Orchid Isle had raised the temperature—and the stakes.

If only he wasn't her boss…Cheryl knew she would be in his arms right now. The thought of it was heaven and hell all at once. The only thing she wanted in life was Marco, but surrendering to him would never bring her happiness. She knew he would only toy with her heart. She ran a hand across her feverish brow. To be seduced by him was a dream, but one that could so easily turn into a nightmare. Only one thing could really stop it coming true. Marco always claimed to have Vettor's best interests at heart. Distracting the little boy's top-class nanny was not the way to do that. Cheryl might doubt that Marco had a heart, but he definitely had brains. With luck, he would go on using them to stop her making a fool of herself.

The light of lust had dimmed in his eyes before he turned away, but Cheryl didn't take any comfort from that. With one last longing look at him, she tried to harden her heart. There was a paradise of clothes in front of her. It was no substitute for being in Marco's arms, but it would have to do.

Cheryl opened the door of her apartment, stopped and breathed in deeply. Then she stood and stared. That lovely new fabric smell, magnified a hundred times, was combined with a wonderful sight. Her lounge was filled with racks of clothes. The colour and quality of things on offer was beyond her wildest dreams.

She wandered from one end of the hanging racks to the other, and then back. Now and again she raised her hand to touch a silken skirt or sleeve. Each time she stopped herself actually making contact. Any one of these items must cost more than she spent on clothes in a whole year. How could she dare choose a single thing knowing that?

It was a long time before her brain forced her to do as she'd been told. First and foremost, Marco was her boss. He said she needed clothes and he was willing to provide them for her. The least she could do was try to find some. And, after all, this wasn't some terrible form of torture. It was shopping, for goodness' sake!

She decided to go for the cheapest items. This was easy in theory, but bracing herself to hunt for price tags was almost impossible. The items were light as gossamer, and she was afraid of damaging anything. She soon discovered there were no prices to find, but the ripple of fine fabric beneath her fingertips worked wonders. Once she began touching things, one spell was broken and another one cast. Thinking back to what Marco had suggested she would need, she picked out the minimum number of things.

When it came to swimwear, 'minimum' was all there was on offer. Much of the selection consisted of nothing more than tiny thongs laced around coat hangers. There were no bra tops. Cheryl was self-conscious enough in her boring old uniform. Going topless in front of Marco Rossi would be a fantasy too far. Moving farther along the rail, she found bikinis. These were so tiny the first wave would wash them away. The least revealing item was a silver one-piece with a racing back and minimal front. In desperation, Cheryl tried it on.

One look in her bathroom mirror and she sighed. It wasn't only with relief. The swimming costume looked wonderful, skimming her curves with the exotic glitter of a salmon. Cheryl never expected to look good in clothes, so this was a real surprise. Ill-fitting chainstore items in cheap fabrics were a world away from this heaven in a five-star dressing room. Working for Marco was showing her how life could be, and it was good.

She could hardly bear to take the swimming costume off, but there was more choosing to be done. By this time Cheryl was fired with enthusiasm. She ran her hands over luxuries she had never seen before and would never experience again. Moirés, silks and satins in every colour from burgundy to white sparkled and begged her to choose. Eventually she settled on a long, sleeveless white dress, splashed with one vivid cerise peony. Its skirt was split daringly high, but a matching high-necked jacket made it the least revealing gown on offer.

For possibly the first time in her life Cheryl was enjoying the sight of herself in a mirror. She added some silver stilettos from a selection of shoes on offer and twirled around like a queen—until there was a knock at the door.

'Who is it?'

'Me.'

There was no mistaking Marco's deep authoritative voice. 'Have you made your choice yet?'

'Yes, I have.'

'Good. I'm here to offer you my unbiased opinion.'

'Unbiased?' she repeated, trying to convince herself as she moved towards the door.

'Well, as unbiased as any Italian man can be when it comes to women.'

There was a confident lilt in his voice, and through the louvre door of her apartment Cheryl saw his silhouette make a gesture that clearly meant *Well, what can you expect?*

She realised a smile was creeping up on her. She stopped it straight away. Marco sounded relaxed enough, but she knew men could change in an instant. Life with Nick had taught her never to trust appearances. Then she caught sight of herself in a nearby mirror. This dress showed off a generous amount of cleavage. Putting the jacket on, she fastened each tiny pearl button from waist to neck. Then she opened the door, bracing herself for the blaze of Marco's scrutiny.

Lounging against the exterior wall, he was looking down towards the beach. The sight of her in the white silk evening dress had an instant effect on him. He stood up straight. His eyes opened wide with amazement and his grin became a long, slow whistle.

'That is some dress,' he breathed.

Cheryl spread her arms and looked down. It certainly was beautiful. The exquisite fabric rustled around her slender body with a sigh that was echoed by Marco.

'Turn around. I want to see it all,' he commanded. Meekly, Cheryl did as she was told. She pirouetted slowly under his gaze. All the time she could feel the sear of his scrutiny running over her, loving every centimetre.

'*Very* nice,' he said at last.

The warmth he gave those two simple words transformed them. Although she was nervous, Cheryl risked a direct look at him when she heard that. His expression had a magical effect on her. Critically, his interest was centred on the dress, not her. That gave her the self-confidence to glow. He looked genuinely impressed.

'So you like it?' She flicked out the material of the dress. It swept down from her fingers like an avalanche.

'You'll outshine any woman who dares to come near you. Does it work?'

Cheryl frowned. 'What do you mean?'

'Can you dance in it?'

In one sinuous movement Marco slid an arm around her waist. He swept her into her apartment, off her feet—and onto his. Half a dozen steps in her new silver stilettos convinced them both Cheryl was no dancer. She stumbled and fell into him.

'This is our first meeting all over again.' He chuckled softly into her ear. Her cheeks pinkened with a rush of guilty pleasure. He supported her, and showed no signs of letting go. Despite the feeling she must be leaving prints all over Marco's bare feet, Cheryl let him carry on. This chance to feel his arms around her one more time made her reckless, and she laughed.

'Oh, dear. I'm sorry, Marco!'

'Don't be,' he murmured. 'I can't expect you to be absolutely perfect in everything. And after all, dancing isn't part of your job description.'

*Oh, how I wish it was*, Cheryl thought. It would be the perfect excuse to accept his arms around her at any time, without any consequences.

He stopped. Dreading the loss of his touch, Cheryl shivered. Far from letting her go, Marco's hands closed around her body.

'How can you be cold at a time like this, *cara*?' He drew

her closer to him, enfolding her with those strong arms she had fantasised about from their very first meeting.

'I'm not,' she whispered, her cheek almost brushing the smooth bronze skin of his shoulder.

'But you're trembling as much as you were the night that storm threw you into my arms.' He spoke gently. 'Why? You've worked for me for long enough to know I'm not the monster people say.'

Cheryl had no answer to that—but Marco did.

'If I was so terrible, would I do this to you?'

He lowered his head. She tensed. Then slowly, sweetly, came the moment she had been waiting for. His lips made contact with hers. The warmth that bubbled through her whenever he was near became a boiling wave of passion. Carried along by the pressure of his kiss, Cheryl swept her arms around his practically naked body. She clung to his stability as her mind spun in a whirlpool of desire.

She had imagined his kiss long into her lonely nights. Now it was actually happening. It was better than anything her most fevered dreams had brought. Her hands roamed over the smooth expanse of Marco's muscular body. She delighted in feeling the change in texture from smooth skin to the soft downy hair of his chest. As she moulded herself to him, he pressed himself against her with delicious insistence. Cheryl could not believe a kiss could be so wonderful. His strength brought nothing but reassurance. Although there was no mistaking the power of his arousal as it nuzzled against her, the sensation filled her with excitement, not fear.

Desperate to experience every inch of him, she clung on. But it wasn't to be. Just as her mind started to leave her body altogether, he peeled away from her.

'That should have warmed you up, *bella*!' he said, with a wolfish smile on his face.

Pink and breathless, Cheryl gazed at him. She was speechless. It was incredible. He could turn off the heat as easily as he could turn her on. Now he was getting ready to leave, as if nothing had happened...

'So, now I've given my approval to your evening wear, change into your new swimming things and meet us on the beach.' He went on, already opening the door to go, 'There's no point in coming to an island paradise if you aren't going to experience the sea.'

*And no point in your kisses, either. They're nothing more than a game to you, are they, Marco?* Cheryl thought, burning with frustration as he walked away.

She spent the whole of that day either in the sea or on the beach. All the time she was supervising Vettor, she was painfully conscious of Marco. His computer had been set up in the shade of some palm trees, with a good view of the ocean. Although she never caught him looking at her, she sensed he was keeping a watchful eye on them both. She took it as a small sign that he really did care for Vettor, deep down, even if he didn't care for her at all. That went some way to softening the disappointment of his meaningless kiss. She was willing to make almost any sacrifice if things turned out all right between Marco and his nephew.

Late in the afternoon, one of Marco's staff splashed up to them with a summons. When Vettor asked to be swung up onto the errand boy's shoulders for the jog back up the beach, Cheryl was delighted. The sad little boy from Monteolio was coming on well. She was happier still when Marco told them why he'd called them back to the complex.

'My barman has invented this cocktail in Vettor's honour. He's kept the recipe a secret, but it's non-alcoholic, of course. I suspect it contains a healthy dose of ugli fruit juice.'

'Ugli fruit? I don't know if I like the sound of that.' Cheryl sounded doubtful.

'It's been given that name to keep it unpopular. That means there's all the more for us.' Marco gave her a knowing smile.

He watched Vettor take a sip of the golden juice. The little boy considered, licked his lips, and then drained the whole glass in one go. With a great gasp of satisfaction, he wiped one sandy hand across his face. Then he set off back towards the sea.

Cheryl instantly started after him, but Marco laid a hand on her arm. Signalling for one of his staff to take care of Vettor, he turned the full power of his charm on her.

'It gets Vettor's seal of approval. Now it's your turn. Ugli fruit is a cross between a tangerine and a grape-fruit—more refreshing than one parent, but not as sour as the other. Try a little straight.'

He motioned to his barman, who placed a glass loaded with ice in front of Cheryl. A cascade of fragrant fruit juice crackled over the cubes. Savouring a mouthful, she found it tasted as good as it looked. He smiled at her expression. It was an innocent enough gesture, so Cheryl risked bringing up a sensitive subject.

'I'd like to thank you for arranging everything, Marco. The clothes you provided for me are truly lovely.' She looked away. 'Unfortunately…I'm afraid I don't actually have any money until pay-day. Certainly not enough for such wonderful things, anyway. Could you arrange to deduct the cost bit by bit from my wages over the next few months?'

Marco could not have been more surprised if she had strolled up from the sea stark naked. Rocking back in his chair, he gazed at her, incredulous.

'You are *still* offering to pay me?'

The shock of his reaction alarmed Cheryl more than a demand for money would have done.

'But of course—I must! You can't be expected to buy things for me!'

Marco's lips compressed with disbelief.

'Of course I can.' He shook his head, uncomfortable for a second. Then his expression became enigmatic again. 'You'll only be wearing these clothes while you're in my employment, won't you? That means they count as working clothes. So I'm supplying them as your employer.'

When Cheryl thought of it like that, she felt slightly better. But it wouldn't be right to agree instantly, so she pursed her lips. When she spoke again she tried to sound dubious.

'Well…as long as you're *sure*.'

'I'm positive.'

Cheryl relaxed a little. She couldn't guess how much the things she had picked out from those racks might cost. To know she wasn't going to be charged for them was a real relief. She took another sip of her juice. It tasted even better without the shadow of debt hanging over her.

'It seems a shame to add other things to this and make it into a cocktail.'

Marco grimaced. 'Don't let Andreas hear you say that. He considers himself a real *artiste* when it comes to mixing drinks.'

'What *would* your friends on the building sites say to hear you talking like that?' Cheryl slipped in slyly between more sips of her drink.

'I dread to think,' Marco muttered, but with none of the humour she expected.

'Do you miss it?'

'Yes. Yes, I do.'

It was a gut reaction, and instantaneous. Marco looked as surprised by his reply as Cheryl had been by her own impulsive question.

'Then why don't you go back to it?'

His astonishment morphed into caution. He narrowed his eyes.

'Nobody has ever said anything like that to me before.'

Something about the gentle breeze and the relaxing sigh of the sea lulled Cheryl into saying far more than she would have risked at home. 'Anyone who has watched you working at that laptop can see it's not doing you any good, Marco. You crouch over it in a way that must make your head ache. And the things you call it! If looks could kill… I'm amazed your screen doesn't burst into flames.'

Her exasperation grew as she remembered something she had seen only a couple of days earlier. 'But when you got that huge shard of wood in your finger you pulled it out without a mention. Office work is hurting you far more—I can tell. It isn't worth a heart attack, Marco. But making a home for Vettor's chickens? Now, that's *well* worth a splinter or two.'

He gazed at her with clouded wonder. Then he looked down at his hands again, turning them over to search for damage. Eventually he spotted a small scab, and chuckled.

'You remembered that? I don't recall doing it at all. Scrapes like that come with the job. They aren't so bad when your hands are toughened to the work. But these days? *Inferno!* I have the hands of an office worker.'

He continued to stare at his hands, rubbing the pads of his thumbs and fingers over each other in a gesture Cheryl recognised. She could see the distaste in his eyes. He was feeling the delicacy in his fingertips that so delighted her.

'Even pen-pushers must have holidays.' Cheryl sighed, watching Vettor and his new friend splashing in the shallows. After a while, an idea came to her.

'Vettor can't swim,' she said idly. 'I wish I was good enough to teach him. He loves paddling so much. It would be safer, and give him a lot more confidence, if someone could be found to give him proper lessons.'

Marco turned away and tried to concentrate on his computer. Cheryl saw the effort it took. He kept on staring at the screen, but without doing anything. Working on automatic, the display constantly refreshed itself. *Sucking the life out of him*, she thought bitterly.

There was a long silence. Eventually he pushed his chair back from his workstation. Arms outstretched, he flexed his shoulders in a ripple of power before relaxing his neck in a graceful arc. As Cheryl watched, the shackles of business fell away, taking a decade of stress from his face.

'*Mio Dio!* Who could work on a day like this?'

He slapped his hands on the tabletop and stood up.

'Take the rest of the day off to enjoy yourself, Cheryl. I shall be taking care of Vettor for a while.'

# CHAPTER EIGHT

ALTHOUGH there was a fitness suite, the natural pool and jungle walks to enjoy, Cheryl didn't spend her spare time on any of them. She sat in the shade of a palm tree sipping ugli juice, watching Marco and Vettor in the clear blue water. *It's a role I was born to play*, she thought. *Watching other people enjoying themselves.* All her life she had been insulated from other people by a bubble of self-consciousness. She could never risk breaking out to engage with other people. Unlike Marco, who was soon splashing about in the sea without a care in the world.

It felt like hours later when Marco finally strode up the beach, trailing his nephew by the hand. Passing Vettor's small wet paw over to Cheryl, he accepted a beach towel from one of his staff.

'*Eccellente.*' He rubbed himself dry with enthusiasm.

It was infectious. Cheryl began to simmer with the nearness of him. She swept a bathsheet around Vettor's shoulders, trying to blot out the image of sea-splashed, sandy Marco. As she did so she heard Marco's deep accent calling for someone to take his nephew off to bed. Before sending him away, Marco ruffled the little boy's hair and Vettor looked up adoringly. Cheryl was so pleased that at last Marco was letting his nephew into his life—putting the past behind him and allowing himself to care. She could see the fondness he had developed for the boy and noticed how much more relaxed they were together. Almost like father and son now.

When Marco spoke again, a warm breeze of sensation fanned the ashes of Cheryl's desire right back into life. It didn't matter what he said. It was the sound of his voice that bewitched her.

'You didn't feel like getting your new swimsuit wet again after all, Cheryl?'

'I didn't want to spoil your fun. I can't swim well enough to enjoy horseplay.'

He looked at her pensively. 'There's still an hour or so of daylight left. Why don't you join me in the water for a swim now my staff have taken charge of Vettor?'

'I don't know…' Cheryl held back.

Marco misunderstood, and his smile warmed.

'There'll be no splashing, guaranteed. It'll set the scene perfectly for dinner. And if we get the timing right we can enjoy a show as we eat. As I said, Orchid Isle sunsets are an unmissable sight.'

Cheryl's heart was singing as she went to her apartment to change. First Marco had abandoned work for play, and now he was pulling her out of her bubble of isolation for a glimpse of his world. Miracles could happen, after all.

Cheryl's new swimming costume looked every bit as spectacular as she remembered. At the last moment she realised she wasn't brave enough to walk about on dry land dressed so scantily. Luckily, silk robes were supplied in each of Marco's guest suites. She slipped on a vivid fuchsia and purple sarong, and started for the sea.

It felt like a long walk through the Orchid Isle complex. Cheryl's heartbeat increased with every step. Soon it was almost as loud as the forest. All around her the churr of insects and the exotic warble of birds throbbed like a wild pulse. Reaching the hem of trees skirting the beach, she stopped. The water was deserted, the sun-shadowed waves breaking on an empty expanse of shore.

'One of your favourite fruit juices, fresh from the press.'

Marco's voice purred up from behind her. It almost sent her into orbit.

'You frightened me to death!'

'You're looking very well on it.' The corners of his mouth lifted. Sipping his own drink, he handed over her glass. 'How is Vettor?'

'He's sound asleep, with a smile on his face.'

Cheryl took the fruit juice from him, resisting the temptation to press its freezing glass against her burning cheeks. A satisfied smile spread over Marco's face. In that instant Cheryl realised he'd planned this all along.

'So *that's* why you took him swimming. It was a deliberate attempt to wear him out!'

'Yes, but it turned out to be more fun than I'd imagined.' His eyes sparkled with laughter, while his hands idly wiped away the droplets of water that their glasses had left on the bar.

'Thank you, Marco. It was a great idea,' she said, full of feeling.

Picking up on her tone of voice, he stopped what he was doing and shot her a knowing look.

'You see? We men have our uses.'

'I've never doubted it.'

Cheryl used a cocktail stick to fish a sliver of cantaloupe from her drink. She nibbled it, trying to give the impression that this was just another conversation in just another bar. But her eyes were everywhere, taking in details. There were solid silver name plates beneath every bottle on display, and porcelain dishes of snacks sitting beneath individual glass domes. This was a universe away from dusty bar snacks at her local pub.

'Really? You sometimes give the impression you don't like men very much.'

He sounded almost understanding. Cheryl hesitated. It would be such a relief to confide in someone. But how could she possibly tell Marco what a fool she'd been? Her parents continually reminded her of the hideous mess she'd made of her life. If blood relatives could do that, how would her employer react? She ran her finger around the sugar-encrusted rim of her glass. The hard, rough edge spoiled its sweetness for her. It reminded her of life.

'It's because something happened, way back in my past,' she told Marco with difficulty. 'I was a fool to expect a happy-ever-after, that's all. It won't happen again. Do you mind if we—'

'Change the subject?' Marco said smoothly.

They exchanged a look and Cheryl got another shock. She saw something new in his cool blue gaze. It wasn't lust or curiosity. It was almost as though he understood exactly how she felt.

'Not at all,' he added with a lazy smile that wasn't mirrored in his eyes. 'Let's swim instead.'

Taking her glass and the cocktail stick from her, he placed them on the bar next to his own. Reaching out his hand, he waited for Cheryl to accept it. She hesitated, but only for a second. Dropping her sarong and towel on the nearest barstool, she took his hand, holding her breath, nervous of his reaction to the revealing swimsuit.

'What do you think?' she said shyly.

There was a heavy pause as his eyes roamed her semi-naked body. 'You look wonderful.'

A blush spread across Cheryl's cheeks as he led her into the warm water. It was paradise. As Cheryl sank into the sea's fluid embrace, her awkwardness dissolved. There was still enough daylight left to pierce the shallows. She could look down on glorious shoals of reef fish. Snappers and parrot fish flitted around displays of every type of coral. There were delicate fans, brittle as brandy snaps, pillows that looked like meringue but were hard to the touch, and a miniature garden in candy colours. Cheryl felt like a child in a sweet shop.

'That was the most beautiful thing I've ever seen in my life!' she gasped, as they finished their swim and started wading back towards the beach.

'I wouldn't say that.' Marco gazed down at her, his expression dark and sensual.

When it came to women, he acted on instinct. He never planned, but events were definitely nudging him in a particular direction. Cheryl was attracted to him. That much had been obvious from their first meeting. He'd stopped short of seduction up until now, but things were changing. Their chat just before swimming had told Marco one very important thing. Cheryl had been hurt in the past. She knew how it felt to give her heart and have it shattered. It wasn't something she wanted to happen again any more than he did. She would be wary of commitment. That was how Marco liked his women. He smiled to himself. A little seduction would make a perfect start to his holiday.

When it came to sex, Marco was highly selective. He could go for months with only work to sustain him. But when an unmissable opportunity like this arose—well, he wasn't a monk. By bringing Cheryl here he had gambled that his rule against bedding his staff would stop him being tempted. Tonight it was a different matter. Sun, sea, sand and most especially her shining swimsuit made all bets void.

*Why not?* he thought. After a bad experience, Cheryl wouldn't want commitment. And he didn't want to sleep alone. They were the ingredients for the perfect holiday romance. Orchid Isle was a place where they could both forget their pain. For a few magic moments it could be replaced with pleasure.

He looked down at her with a slow, sweet smile.

'Cheryl,' he said quietly. 'What you said before we went into the sea…it's been troubling me. You and I may have had our misunderstandings, but I wouldn't like you to think I was totally unfeeling.'

She shrugged. 'It sounds as though you've had a hard life. It must have toughened you.'

'There's been nothing I can't handle,' he said, trying not to think back too carefully, or too far.

He took another step, as though heading back to the bar. Cheryl started to follow, but he had already stopped again. Now they were standing much closer together than before.

Something about the setting sun and the gentle breeze turned her heart to butter.

'Tell me, Marco,' she said softly.

Gazing along the sweep of the bay, he shook his head. 'Another time, maybe. It doesn't matter.'

'Yes, it does.'

In an impulsive gesture, Cheryl's hand went out and touched his arm. The circuit between them was complete.

Slowly, he turned to face her properly, and he murmured, 'That wonderful kiss we shared…it wasn't enough for me.'

She had been gazing up into his face, her eyes full of concern. When he said that she lowered her lids. Her lips parted, but the only sound came from the surging surf on the shore. Marco raised his hand. With a touch that was no touch at all, his fingertips traced a droplet of seawater as it ran from her hair down the plane of her cheek. When he reached her chin, he lifted it. At the same time his thumb smoothed away her worries. Cheryl closed her eyes.

Their first caresses were slow, soft and subtle. Marco was in no rush. Anticipation was almost as sweet as the act itself. He knew exactly where his first kiss was going to lead. It was inevitable. This affair had been destined from the moment they met. Like all women, Cheryl would be powerless to resist him. That flimsy swimming costume would slide off, and she would be his. Her lissom little body would mould itself beneath the warmth of his fingers. His hands would roam over her peach-smooth skin, relishing every curve, until finally, wet and willing, she would straddle her legs in an unmistakable invitation for him to seek out the most intimate parts of her—

'No!'

He stopped and drew back from her. Silence fell between them.

Cheryl had never experienced such absolute stillness before. Far out in the bay, the setting sun touched the horizon. It was so quiet she waited, as if for the hiss of flames touching water. Then, after an agonising pause, the hand that was encircling her began to weave a dancing pattern over her shoulder again. His slow movements were as light as shadows drifting over her skin.

'What is it, *tesoro*?'

The whisper of his voice was as insubstantial as his touch. Cheryl took a deep breath. She tried to hold it, but couldn't. It escaped in a shuddering sigh. She tried again. Wordlessly, Marco's touch became slower and still more gentle. Eventually, his patience gave her the courage to speak.

'I—I don't do sex,' she said at last. His caress became a pat of reassurance, and she let her breath go in a gasp of relief.

'But that was just a kiss.' He smiled, his eyes dark with heady passion.

Cheryl stiffened. 'In my experience, one thing leads to another.'

'And in mine.'

She was withdrawing from him. Marco was having none of it. He gathered her unyielding body back into his arms.

'Something bad has happened to you in the past,

Cheryl. I sensed it from the moment we met. And the way you backed off from those workmen confirmed what I already thought.' His voice grew molten. 'But this time will be different. I promise you.' His vow was so powerful it silenced her with a whisper. 'Believe me. I know how to treat a woman—especially a delicate little flower like you. Forget everything except here and now. You are safe with me. I told you so when you first threw yourself into my arms that night at the Villa Monteolio. Remember?'

How could she forget? The memory of his calm strength melted into the warm reality of his hands. All the panic ebbed from her body.

Marco felt the subtle change as her shoulders softened. She didn't feel threatened any more. The only thing between them now was an unspoken understanding. Nothing was going to happen—unless she wanted it.

In a confusion of emotion, Cheryl had never felt so secure, and yet so apprehensive. This second, this minute was wonderful. But when the time came, what then?

'I'll take care of you.' His voice held all the warmth of the sea as he murmured into her hair.

'It isn't that I don't want to,' Cheryl murmured, 'especially with you. It's just that…I can't believe you could want me.' She closed her eyes and rested her brow against his chest. Unable to see his face, she felt him lift his head, but did not see the frown troubling his features.

When he spoke again, there was no hint of what might have been going through his mind.

'No man alive could resist the silent temptation you've been to me since we first met, Cheryl.' His delicious accent caressed her name like liquid silver, 'I'm stalked by so many women, and they are only interested in what they can get out of me. But you—you are different. Your feelings are shown so clearly, and your body betrays you. I know you must be as innocent as I am experienced. Let me show you all the pleasure at my fingertips…'

His last words whispered away into the curve between her neck and shoulder. Cheryl was a willing prize. She closed her eyes, surrendering totally to the strong arms that surrounded her.

Their kiss drove everything from her mind except the touch and taste of him. Suspended in an orb of passion, time seemed to stand still. But when at last he gently pulled away from her, a sliver of moon had risen above the shadowy hills of Marco's own kingdom.

Cheryl shivered. Marco was in charge here. *This is his domain so there's no escape*, she thought. *I'd better get it over and done with, and let him decide what happens next. He is judge and jury in his own land.*

'I never know what to do…to say…' she whispered, hardly able to get the words out.

Marco caressed her face, then ran his hands through her thick hair. 'That isn't the brave girl who stood between me and Vettor at our first meeting!'

'I didn't know who you were then,' she replied, adding to herself, *Only what a man of your size and strength might be capable of.*

Cheryl was torn. She knew what Marco was like, and how many women he had bedded. Why would it be different for her? Could she trust him with her body? With her heart?

'Tell me, Cheryl. Tell me what happened in the past to make you so wary. You are like a frightened child.'

He held her close as he spoke. She could feel the vibrations of his voice through his chest and the sensation comforted her.

It took a long time. Eventually, she sighed again and said, 'I've always been different—right from the start. My parents were so proud when I got to grammar school. I worked hard, and got top grades in everything,' she told him. 'There was nothing else to do. I had no friends. No, really—it's true. My parents said we were too poor to mix with families from the grammar school side of town.'

Marco gritted his teeth, holding her tighter.

They were both silent for a while. Then Cheryl plucked up the courage to go on.

'College was just as lonely. I buried myself in my books. And the Internet,' she added heavily.

'I think I can see where this is going.' Marco grimaced. 'You met up with someone you'd been chatting to online, and had a bad experience?'

She nodded. 'His name was Nick Challenger. When I told him how miserable I was at home he sympathised. He really was the perfect friend—to begin with. We met, and at the time I thought there was electricity between us. Now I know better.'

She thought back to her first meeting with Marco. That was *real* attraction. If only she'd been able to recognise the fake in Nick. Two tears escaped from her eyes.

'Oh, *mio tesoro*…' he whispered, stroking the tears from her cheeks.

'P-please don't be kind to me. I can't stand it!' she sobbed.

'Yes, you can. While you are here with me I will let no one hurt you.'

Although she could hardly see out of her raw eyes, she looked into his. Expecting to see pity, all she saw was concern.

'I must look awful,' she snivelled, but he squeezed her hands. Then it didn't matter any more.

'Do you think I care about that? Believe me. You are good and kind. Nothing and no one can take that away from you. Instead they should treat you as the delicate treasure you are. You deserve the best that life can offer, Cheryl. Never forget that,' he whispered, before gently placing another kiss on her lips.

# CHAPTER NINE

CHERYL was in love. In a rush of emotion, she realised this was the real thing. Heat and hormones had fired her feelings for the past few weeks. But this was something new: a deep, calm assurance. The comfort Marco was giving her had set the seal on it. He cared for her, when she had no one. He was the only man in the world who made her feel like this and treated her so well. Her self-esteem had been at a low ebb. With a few well-chosen words Marco was restoring it, moment by moment. He didn't care about her track record.

If anyone had suggested that a few hours ago, she would have thought it was because he didn't care about *her*. Now she could dare to hope. Perhaps he did care but, being the man he was, the only way he could show it was by letting her know the past didn't matter to him.

For a few glorious moments Cheryl let herself dream. Marco Rossi was not the sort to lay his feelings open for all to see. She went back over every second they had shared together, from the time they'd got out of the water. It was glorious. Surely he couldn't kiss her like this unless it meant something? And all this concern for her…

To Cheryl, a little of Marco's business armour had

been rubbed away. She had glimpsed the real man, and he was worth a thousand others. From now on she would do anything he asked. He had so much, when all she had was her loyalty. So when Marco took her hand, he made her the happiest woman alive.

He led her over to some tall trees fringing the beach. When she saw a hammock suspended between two of the palms, her footsteps hesitated.

'Stay with me, Cheryl.' Marco's voice was deep with authority. 'You shouldn't be alone. And I want you near me tonight.'

She moved forward with slow, silent acceptance. Despite her past, this was a new beginning. Marco had told her so. She couldn't have resisted even if she had wanted to.

He secured the wide, softly padded sling and then drew her in beside him. 'Nothing will happen.' His voice was a low caress. 'Unless you want it to, *tesoro*.'

Cheryl allowed herself to settle down against him. Leaning against Marco like this was a perfect fantasy. It drove all other thoughts from her mind—except one. What if he turned out to be exactly the same as Nick? Lulling her into trust and abandonment in the same way he'd eased her into this hammock?

Her body tightened with apprehension.

'Rest here, against my neck.' He cupped his hand around her head and drew her gently in towards his body.

'What if I say I don't want to?'

His touch glided away, freeing her.

'Then that's fine. I don't need to prove anything.'

Cheryl hesitated. This time it was more because she was afraid of what she might do, rather than what

Marco might have in mind. The warm scent of the sea rose from him like an invitation. He stayed perfectly still, waiting. At last Cheryl could not resist any longer. She sank down beside him again and the hammock rolled them gently together, skin against naked skin.

Marco didn't move, allowing her to come to him. When she let out a long, satisfied sigh he laid one arm around her, letting it fall casually down the length of her curled body. She felt the faint rasp of wind-dried salt on his skin as he enfolded her. At the same time his voice teased her with slow, caressing whispers of reassurance. It was a tone guaranteed to keep her in his arms for as long as he wanted. Cheryl was content to stay there for ever.

When his hands drifted from her hair to her shoulders and then moved to the sleek sides of her swimming costume, they both knew there was no going back. No woman could resist the temptation of him. Cheryl stretched beneath him, eager to feel his touch over every inch of her body. Once again his fingers found their way beneath the soft stretchy fabric. Caressing the smooth skin of her derriere with one hand, he drew her gently in to another kiss with the other.

'See, *innamorata*? I'm not the monster you thought.' His voice was like moonlight on the water.

'But what if…if…?' Cheryl hesitated, afraid of saying what was in her heart in case it made him stop.

Marco put his head on one side. 'You wanted me to stop? I would. It's up to you. You're a free agent. Just like me. Either one of us could get up and go at any time.'

'Oh, no!' Cheryl saw her worst nightmare coming true. That he would leave her even now.

'But I'm not going anywhere.' His lips parted in another slow, seductive smile.

'And I don't want to go.' Cheryl glanced back at the complex. But what would people think if she stayed? How could she use her position as Vettor's nanny like this? She bit her lip. 'But…'

'Then stay.' He withdrew his fingers from her panty line. Skipping them lightly up the length of her body, he began toying with the thin straps of her swimming costume.

His every movement set her nerves dancing. Gradually, his caresses stroked away every thought of anything outside the universe within his arms.

'Making love is the greatest pleasure known to man. Why would I want to keep you in my arms by force?' he murmured.

'You'll never need to do that.' Her eyes were large, and dark with trust. 'I want this, Marco, but…I don't know how. Not properly…and what happens if I'm no good at it?'

He made a sound of pure disbelief.

'Do you think that matters to me? A man gets his pleasure no matter what. I can wait…though not for ever.'

His voice was a growl of happy anticipation. It set free a primitive urge within Cheryl. Her mouth was parched, but she didn't need to talk any more. They kissed until all that mattered was the sensation of being totally absorbed in one another. When Marco finally released her body to question her expression, she raised a hand straight to his cheek.

'Please don't stop…'

Everything from the sweet huskiness of her voice to her fawn-light touch combined to make Cheryl totally desirable in Marco's eyes.

'*Tesoro…*' he murmured, drawing her gently, easily back into his arms. The next moment her face was pressed against his shoulder, held there by the warm security of his hand. 'You don't mind?'

She shook her head.

Slipping a finger beneath her chin, he raised her head. Looking straight into her eyes, he murmured, 'Then this is how it will be.'

Once more his kisses were soft and sweet against her lips. His gentle longing inspired Cheryl. She responded again, tentatively at first, and then let desire send her hands around him. She encircled his waist, feeling the vital glow of his naked skin.

'I shall teach you how to love,' he whispered. 'But it is a skill that takes many, many lessons. Don't feel you have to take them all at once.'

Cheryl lost herself within his sheltering arms. She had never felt so loved. *No!* she brought herself up short. *Love isn't one of his words.*

'It's a skill,' he murmured, nibbling down the length of her neck. 'Honed by years of practice.'

His voice was indistinct, but Cheryl thought she heard amusement in it. He wasn't laughing at her, was he? She tensed, but in that same instant Marco transferred his attention to her earlobe. Suddenly nothing else mattered. Her body dissolved. All the support she needed was there, coming straight from him.

'Would you really stop now, if I asked you to?' she gulped.

He stopped anyway. The instant he did, Cheryl wished she hadn't said anything.

'Of course.' He was watchful, quizzing her with his eyes. 'But you don't really want me to, do you?'

In reply, Cheryl reached up and began their next kiss. Then Marco took back the initiative. Peeling off her swimming costume, he encouraged her to strip him, too. Unrestricted, their bodies twined in a dance of ecstasy.

Cheryl lost track of time as he worshipped every inch of her. Then, when she was faint with pleasure, he drew her to the greatest peak of all. Gasping, she accepted his body as he sank forward. Gripped in the velvet of her embrace, Marco took a few seconds to master his instincts. They were almost overwhelming. But he wanted this to be a time for her, not him. Gently, with infinite care, he transferred his attention to the creamy sweet skin of her neck, tasting and kissing until the temptation became too great even for him. He drew back, aching for the satisfaction of a second thrust.

'Marco, no…'

He paused, but only until he realised what she meant.

'Marco…no—don't stop…' she pleaded, in a voice he had never expected to hear her use. It was smoky with seduction and totally irresistible. Now it was only the sensation of him leaving her body that caused her to tense.

Her muscles held him as he tenderly cradled her body. Lifting his head from the silken surface of her skin, he looked at her. It was perfection. He sank back into the welcome of her, and she responded with little fluttering cries of pleasure. Her nails dug into his shoulders. She arched beneath him, eyes closed. Marco allowed himself to smile. He loved to see his own special talent at work in a woman. Cheryl would never forget this for as long as she lived. He could guarantee that.

Passion made her more beautiful than ever as he brought her closer and closer to ecstasy. *This is it*, he thought. *She was born to respond like this, and I'm the only man who can inspire it in her.* Then Cheryl cried out his name, setting the seal on their coupling. She called with such longing he couldn't deny her any more. As she gripped his manhood with waves of pleasure, he rose and fell in perfect harmony with her body.

When it was over he started to pull back gently. Cheryl stopped him.

'No! Don't leave me, Marco!'

With a smile, he slid down her body. Nuzzling the tiny bead at the heart of her femininity, he made her sing again with orgasm. When at last her thighs relaxed their iron grip, he raised his head.

'Now, what was it you said about not wanting to do this, *mio tesoro*?'

He reached up and caressed her cheek.

'I didn't want to disappoint you.'

He smiled. 'You didn't.'

Consumed with nerves, Cheryl tried to keep her voice light. In contrast, Marco's movements became heavy. *Is it regret?* she wondered, tentatively reaching out to him. Her fingers slid over his short dark hair. He leaned into her caress, lowering himself down to lie beside her.

'That was incredible,' he breathed.

'You don't mean that.' Cheryl frowned, subsiding against a meringue of cushions.

His attitude changed instantly. 'I don't lie. Particularly about something so important.'

Marco put out his hand to console her. He stopped short of pulling her close to nestle into his body. That would be too intimate. He was starting to realise exactly how much the past few days had meant to him. Over the years, sex had been a regular feature of his life, but no girl had ever touched his heart like this one.

He winced. That was a bad image. He had learned long ago that you couldn't afford the luxury of a heart when it came to women. He reached up with his other hand. Releasing the hammock's brake, he pulled on a silken rope. It set the hammock swinging gently.

The night sky above was sapphire plush, scattered with diamonds. He felt Cheryl's breathing become deeper, slower and more regular. She was asleep.

It was the ultimate sign of her trust in him. There was something about helplessness that always brought out the worst in him. With weak men, he bawled them out and made their working lives a misery. He knew people called him a monster behind his back. He didn't care. Either do a good job or stand aside in favour of someone who can. That was Marco's rule. No, it was his attitude to women that unsettled him. One diamond tear, one tremble, and he was lost.

Marco twisted his head slightly, to look down without disturbing her. She was sleeping like a baby. The long dark lashes sweeping her cheeks emphasised the cool fragility of her English colouring. One small fist rested on his chest. It uncurled as she slipped deeper into sleep. He noticed her fingernails were as pink and perfect as the inside of a seashell. It was a first for him. Usually his interest in a woman's appearance was limited to her face and figure, not the finer details.

He leaned back again to look at the sky. Serenaded by the soft sibilance of insects, he drifted between sleep and wakefulness, cradling Cheryl as she slept. A shooting star scored the blue-black velvet. Wasn't that supposed to mean a baby was being born? He wondered if his poor downtrodden mother had ever seen a meteor. He doubted it. She'd spent all her wretched life at work. Besides, it never got truly dark in the middle of the city.

Cheryl woke from a wonderful dream to find it was all true. She was lying in Marco's arms. A gentle tropical breeze was rocking them. Above her, palm fronds filtered the growing warmth as the sky changed from apricot to peach. The rising sun chased shadows from Marco's face, but not from his expression. That stayed tight-lipped and tense. Cheryl felt a small movement against the softness of her inner thigh. He was aroused again.

It all came rushing back to her—their swim, that kiss, his kindness…

A blush began to rise from somewhere that was as aroused as Marco. What in the world had she done? Sex with Marco had been sublime, but he was her employer, and Vettor's guardian… She swallowed hard, starting to panic. If he woke and regretted their night of passion, it would be unbearable. Out of the corner of her eye she saw her discarded swimsuit, hanging from a branch. That wouldn't be much protection in this paradise, but it was all she had. With the temptation of Marco pressing so insistently against her, it wasn't any help at all. She had to escape.

Her arm was resting against the comfort of his chest. Carefully, millimetre by millimetre, she lifted it clear of the downy curls of his body hair. He didn't move. Hardly daring to breathe, Cheryl grasped the thick over-hanging branch that held her abandoned swimsuit. Gradually transferring her weight from the hammock to the tree, she managed to get out without waking him. Grabbing the sliver of silvery material, she pulled it on.

Her first thought had been to escape before she could see the waking disappointment in his eyes. But now she was dressed, the desire to linger was too strong to resist. She stood on the cool sand for a moment, watching him sleep. It was a spell-binding sight. Marco was so gorgeous, and yet so troubled. She could see it in his face. When awake, he worked hard to keep his emotions secret. Now his inner turmoil was obvious. With one last, lingering look at his beautiful bronze body, she slipped away into the trees.

She went straight to the natural swimming pool. A stream cascaded from a rocky outcrop into a shallow basin, just right for bathing. Every surface was softened with ferns and orchids. Tiny birds flitted through the overhanging trees, lit like shards of stained glass in a green cathedral. Stepping into the water, she felt all her worries wash away. She swam a few leisurely strokes closer to the turbulence created by the cascade. Water foamed and bubbled like a time-lapse film of clouds. It felt heavenly. She dived beneath the surface, fascinated by the tumbling pebbles at the bottom of the pool.

Surfacing through streams of water, the first thing she saw was Marco. He was standing beside an ancient tree, its trunk encrusted with moss, dressed only in his swimming shorts. His body was patterned with the jagged moving shapes of leaf shadows.

'How did you know where I was?'

'It was a lucky guess. I wanted to repay your kindness at Monteolio by bringing you these.' He held up his hands. Her discarded silk sarong lay over one, a soft towel over the other. 'But now I'm here—and you're there, looking like that…'

Smiling, he helped her out of the water. Cheryl wondered why she had ever been afraid of him. If she was nervous now, it was for an entirely different reason. He swirled the towel around her, then stood back to admire the effect.

'If I'd felt you getting up I would have stopped you.'

'Would you? Why? Was something wrong?' She searched his expression.

'No—no, not at all.' His ravishing grin put her mind at ease straight away. 'After last night? And you showed every sign of enjoying it as much as I did.'

'Yes. It was wonderful,' she murmured shyly.

'I told you it would be.'

His confidence was infectious. Cheryl looked up and laughed, but only until she saw the look deep in his blue eyes. Her voice died away as he lifted one end of the towel and began tenderly drying her hair. It was so softly reminiscent of the way he had comforted her the night before that Cheryl gasped.

Marco's expression turned into a slow smile. Scooping the tawny riot of hair back from her face, he ran his fingers through the glossy mane. He was openly admiring everything about her, from the grace of her movements to the beauty of her body. For the first time in her life Cheryl found herself relishing an audience. Marco was the only man she would allow so close. He was everything she needed, now and for ever. Nothing else mattered.

Taking her hand, he led her to a sunlit glade. The forest floor was as soft and yielding as her body.

'This is my idea of paradise,' she breathed, as tropical birds spangled through the canopy of leaves hiding them from the world.

'And mine,' he whispered in response.

His first kiss was long, slow and irresistible. His lips sipped from her, and she was only too willing to respond. The touch of his fingers on her skin was like thistledown drifting on a warm breeze. He took such pleasure in the way she melted against his body that he went on caressing her as they stood in a shaft of filtered sunlight. It was Cheryl who finally drew back a little from him. She looked up at him shyly, but her eyes were limpid with sensuality. Marco's hand went to her hair, tenderly caressing a curl back from her cheek. His smile asked a silent question. Cheryl closed her eyes and lowered her head.

'No—wait.' Marco leaned close to murmur in her ear. 'You're still troubled about something, Cheryl. I can sense it. What's the matter?'

'Nothing.'

'Oh, no—that's not good enough! I've never wanted a woman more than I need you right now,' he whispered. 'But I would walk away rather than coerce you into something you weren't ready for.'

She raised her head and opened her eyes. His expression was penetrating in its honesty. She threw herself against the solid reassurance of his chest. Marco had said he wanted her! In that split second he burst the bubble of isolation separating her from life. He was drawing her towards a whole new future. She could hardly dare hope that happiness would last beyond these few precious moments together. But she could seize her chance and live her dream. If only for a little while…

'I want you, too, Marco—you can't imagine how much. But I'm scared.'

'Not of me?'

She shook her head. When she tried to put her fears of abandonment and pain into words, they came out all wrong.

'I don't know what to do…'

'Then maybe we should consider more lessons…'

With a wolfish grin he pulled her towards him and kissed her with a passion that swept every thought from her mind. In a head-spinning torment of desire, she felt her body warming to him again. Desire bubbled through her veins like champagne. Sliding her arms around his neck, she drew him down onto the soft bed of the forest floor. Hungry for his body, she claimed all his caresses and begged for more. As they lay on the warm yielding surface, he whispered about her beauty and his delight in her body. His fingers traced lascivious lines over her skin, teasing her nipples to peaks of awareness, awakening the coral bead of her femininity with his caresses.

Cheryl was in heaven. She had been unwanted as a child, and unloved as an adult. But in Marco's tropical paradise she became the woman she had always wanted to be. Pulsing with life, tingling with anticipation, she let him lead her towards the greatest prize of all. His lovemaking was slow and intense, teasing every nuance from the union of their bodies. When at last he exploded into her, her fingers dug into the smooth curve of his back in an equally epic orgasm.

Swimming back to earth through a haze of wonderful sensations, they laughed in shared delight. In his spellbinding moment of release, a perfect truth had come to Marco. Sex was something he could take whenever and wherever he fancied it. But what had happened with Cheryl was an entirely new experience for him. In showing her how she could find as much satisfaction as he did in sex, he had discovered something quite different. For the first time in his life, Marco was making love instead of simply luxuriating in sensations.

It was a staggering thought. He lay back, but instead of pulling away from Cheryl he drew her with him. The movement disturbed a tiny jewelled frog. It glittered and was gone in a flash of gold and green. An iridescent butterfly fluttered down and landed on her hair. It was a perfect ornament to her fragile beauty. She was right—this truly was paradise. Desperate not to disturb her, Marco's breath was so light it hardly ruffled the bright blue wings.

And then he felt Cheryl tremble in the silence, and took her in his arms again.

# CHAPTER TEN

'ARE you ready to tell me what was troubling you, Cheryl?' he murmured eventually. She was so completely relaxed now; he knew he had seduced all her immediate worries away.

'It's nothing—no, really!' She smiled and kissed him before he could question her further. 'My past was haunting me, nothing more. I've never had any luck with relationships before. You've been such a shock to my system. I abandoned England to make a fresh start, and I've certainly found one!'

'How do you know you haven't escaped the frying pan by jumping into the fire, *tesoro mio*?' He chuckled.

'Oh, Marco, only you could make me smile at a time like this. To hear you say such an English thing in that beautiful voice of yours—'

'No one's admired my voice before.' He laughed softly and, moving her away from him, held her gaze with his. 'What happened last night, and again just now, could stay a unique experience for both of us. That's up to you. You must decide what is going to happen next, Cheryl. I've wanted you night after night, day after day, but I know my own soul. I'm not interested in emotional ties. I've resisted taking things any further with you until now because I didn't want to hurt your feelings. But anyone who has suffered like you must think the worst of every man right from the start.'

'That's why I work with children,' she said simply. 'They don't know enough about me to inflict pain on purpose.'

'On the other hand, I know too much now.'

'I should never have told you.'

'Yes, you should.' A dark look clouded his features. He frowned, his hands moving restlessly over her body.

'Cheryl, I have a business proposition to put to you. I need a proper, stay-at-home mother for the little one, not a nanny—'

'Oh, you're not going to sack me?' Her face crumpled.

He shook his head, and carried on. 'A woman with your background needs to be sure of a settled, secure future. And I'm in the ideal position to provide both. Marry me, Cheryl.'

It was more than she had ever dreamed of, but she had never expected it to happen in a million years. Her mouth dropped open. For a long time she couldn't say anything. Simply breathing was hard enough. Finally she managed to collect her thoughts and put them into some sort of order.

'I didn't really hear you say that, did I?'

Marco's smile drained. Suddenly, he was the world-beating businessman again. 'It's the obvious solution. I'm a media face who has outgrown all the posing and the press coverage. I don't care what the papers or anyone else say about me any more, but the child is a different matter. I don't want him exposed to gossip. The façade of a happy marriage will keep the gossip columnists off my back and give him the illusion of a normal family life. It will also reward you. For the hell you've suffered in the past, and all the good work you're doing for us now.'

So it wasn't love. For a split second Cheryl might have been able to fool herself, but not any more. Not when Marco could let slip that phrase about *the façade of a happy marriage.*

'This is too sudden—' she began. Marco shrugged her concern aside.

'No, it isn't. I'll get my people to draw up documents to make sure neither of us suffers financially in any way from the arrangement. They'll sort everything out. Everyone will be happy. Think about it—you could go further and fare much worse. And this arrangement would, after all, be strictly business.'

She didn't know what to say. It would be marriage to the only man on earth who made her feel like making love.

'How "strictly" is that, exactly?' she asked doubtfully.

'You mean will I still want sex?' Marco gave a hollow laugh. 'That depends on what my lawyers say. Don't worry, *tesoro*. You haven't minded me ravishing you so far. We are so good together it would be a shame to forgo the bedroom, don't you think?'

Yes, but…'

He laughed, 'Oh, I so love your innocence, Cheryl! That's why this marriage is such a good idea. It puts the

Botox brigade off my tracks, and replaces them with a pretty little original like you.'

Cheryl thought, *but not for long*. Marco was right. Nick had seemed nice, but turned nasty. Marco's terrible public reputation was at odds with the way he could be in private. Appearances could be deceptive— but he was stunning in that department, too. It really was a no-brainer. The man who filled Cheryl's every waking moment and all her dreams was asking her to marry him. It might be a loveless match as far as he was concerned, but Cheryl had enough devotion for all of them. Right then and there, she decided to make sure Marco would never regret it.

'All right, I'll do it,' she announced boldly. 'If arranged marriages are good enough for some royal families, then they're good enough for me.'

From that moment on, Cheryl lived like a queen. They had champagne cocktails and croissants for breakfast. That was followed by a leisurely bath to the sound of birdsong from the surrounding jungle.

As she was deciding what to wear, a masseuse knocked on the door of her apartment. Marco had flown the woman in especially for the occasion. Cheryl had a wonderful time selecting essential oils for the preparation of her own exclusive blend. Then she lay in pampered perfection while every care was soothed away. Much later, softened and supple, she was treated to a succession of wonderful treatments. First a hairdresser, then a reflexologist, a manicurist and finally a beautician came to spoil her.

At first she was desperate to know what Vettor was doing, where he was and who was looking after him.

Gradually her worries receded. Each time someone said *Signor Rossi has taken him down to the beach*, she believed it a little more easily. By the time she was glittering like a superstar, the message was, *Beba has taken him fishing.* When Cheryl stepped out of her apartment, she was totally relaxed and happy. The only thing missing from her life was Marco—and he was the first thing she saw.

He was lounging in the shade of a tree, but stood up as she walked towards him. Cheryl had expected to feel overawed or nervous, but she didn't. The admiration burning in his eyes gave her the confidence to stride out. The billowing folds of her skirt swirled in the warm air, perfuming it with Chanel.

'You look stunning.' He stretched out his hands to her. Drawing her close, he placed a kiss lightly on her forehead.

'Hmm…someone is working well today. I forgot to specify perfume when I arranged everything. They must have remembered my favourite.'

Buoyed up by her luxurious morning, Cheryl put her head on one side. 'Actually, it's my own. I was petrified when I left England to come and work for you. I treated myself to a tiny bottle at the airport as a reward for my own bravery.'

'Then you have exquisite taste.'

He smiled, and Cheryl did the same. If only he knew! Her scent had been chosen because it was the only name she'd recognised. She'd never expected to use it, but this was one of those special occasions she had dreamt about. Now it was here, she was going to enjoy every second.

'I've never felt more pampered,' she sighed, languid with satisfaction. 'Have you two been having fun?' She looked over to where Vettor was investigating a rock pool with one of the errand boys.

'We certainly have. But you and I must get down to business now.'

Cheryl looked back at Marco, her dreams evaporating. *What else could I expect?* she thought grimly. She had never been offered love here, only a job. Even from her first interview for the post of nanny she'd got a hint of what Marco Rossi could be like. Work always came first with him. His absences had told her he had little time for his nephew. This was a man who delegated, rather than loved. No wonder he could offer marriage to her so easily. It was nothing more than a business decision as far as he was concerned. *Well, I can hardly complain about that now*, she told herself. To be fair, he'd never dressed up his proposal as anything but a marriage of convenience. She'd known his reasons before she accepted, and none of them involved love.

'I thought we were supposed to be on holiday.' Pulling away from him, Cheryl strode off down the beach.

'Wait.'

She slowed her footsteps, but only slightly.

'Cheryl.'

His voice gave her name all sorts of meaning. She stopped, digging her toes into the warm silver sand.

'We have things to discuss.'

When she turned around, he was already there. His bare feet had been silent on the sand, but his eyes spoke volumes.

'I'm having my people move your things into my apartment here, and into my suite back at the villa.'

She blinked.

'Is that OK with you?' he added.

It sounded as though he was arranging a business deal.

Cheryl wanted to be romanced, whisked off to bed, made to feel special every time. But who was she to expect things like that?

'I—I suppose so.'

'You don't sound too sure.'

Cheryl looked down at the sand. Tentatively, she put one foot out and rubbed her toes back and forth, drawing a line. Her newly manicured nails glittered like pearls in the sunlight.

'It sounds so clinical when you put it like that,' she managed eventually.

In response to her words Marco strode away up the beach towards the table where his work was laid out in the shade. Her heart plummeted. He really was a businessman to his fingertips. She had agreed to his proposition, and this was how her life was going to be from now on. No romance, just harsh economics.

She watched as he spoke into his mobile phone. Then to her amazement, he dropped the thing. Within seconds he was back at her side.

'You must stop selling yourself short, *tesoro*.' His lilt was questioning.

The fine hair on the back of Cheryl's neck prickled. There was determination in his eyes.

'It's the first rule of business,' he went on. 'Treat yourself as you want others to treat you. Although you needn't think I'm doing any more work today. That phone call was to clear everyone from the far side of the island. They'll all be concentrated around here, ready to fawn on little Prince Vettor while he fishes. That means you and I will have one corner of this paradise all to ourselves.'

His hand slid around her waist. Suddenly Cheryl was in the air, effortlessly swept off her feet. She tried to scream, but only a thin gasp escaped from her throat.

'What are you going to do with me?' Staring at him, wide-eyed with horror, she struggled to speak. The muscles in his arms were like steel hawsers, clenching her against his body.

'Something any intelligent man should have done a long, long time ago.'

He was heading toward the trees. Cheryl could see the waterfall flickering at the far side of the secret glade where he had helped her from the water. Even the forest birds fell silent.

She began to struggle. 'Put me down!'

He laughed. 'What? And get that pretty little pedicure ruined?'

Shouldering his way through fern fronds and palms, Marco carried on regardless. Her prim struggling had no effect on him.

'Stop wriggling—this will be worth it.'

They reached the water's edge. As Marco strode out onto the jetty with Cheryl clamped to his chest, she heard the sound of an engine.

'Right on cue.' A sapphire-blue speedboat swished into dock beside them. Marco thanked the pilot, who leapt out and disappeared towards the complex. 'I won't bother with formalities like tying her up and helping you aboard,' Marco said, and he tossed Cheryl lightly into the boat.

She landed, cat-like, on her feet. As Marco stepped in to join her, she crouched. There was nothing solid to cling to except for the side of the craft—unless she risked grabbing Marco.

Taking the controls, he swung the speedboat around in a wide arc. Pointing its nose down the creek, he headed for the sea.

'You're going to like this, Cheryl.'

'Is that an order?'

He gave her a wry smile, 'No, it's a prediction.'

Taking a pair of sunglasses from a compartment beside him, he put them on. His sure touch on the steering wheel didn't falter.

'Nick was your first boyfriend? Is that right?'

'He was my *only* boyfriend.'

'You've got a lot of catching up to do when it comes to the art of romance. It isn't the sort of thing that can be carried on in the presence of a child. I've arranged for us to take a special lunch at Crystal Bay. There won't be anyone there to disturb us. Not even a waiter. You can carry on learning love from a master.'

Cheryl had to smile—this was beginning to feel like a dream.

A few minutes later, Marco's speedboat rounded the coast on the other side of his island. Crystal Bay was protected from onshore breezes, and the still air was heavy with the fragrance of tropical flowers. Its silvery curve of beach was absolutely deserted. Marco nosed the launch towards a newly built jetty. A cloud of pretty parakeets scattered through the trees with a noise like thrown jewels. After tying up the boat, he stepped ashore and reached for Cheryl's hand.

'You need me, Cheryl. Let me show you how things should be between a man and a woman.'

Before she could think what to say, he pointed towards a belt of trees beyond the beach. Following the line of his arm, she noticed a wooden chalet with a thatched roof, well camouflaged among the dappled shade of the trees.

'What do you think?' he carried on, without waiting for her reply. 'I want to make up for our first date last night being so…unconventional. Lunch today will be our chance to get to know each other. You know what they say…there should be one date for every decade of your age before the man suggests—' he gave that lopsided grin of his which always made Cheryl forget her worries '—in my case *marriage*.'

To her amazement, Cheryl found herself smiling right back at him. Her mind raced, already filling with ideas. Marco might be treating their arranged marriage as a sham, but he was the man of her dreams. Who else would do something like this for her? He really was perfect. What more could she want?

*A proper wedding*, she told herself. Gradually, she realised part of the solution might be in her own hands. Marriage to Marco ought to be a cause for celebration. What better reason could there be for treating herself? The lives of her parents had taught her one important thing. Mr and Mrs Lane had always spent every penny of their money. They liked to treat themselves whenever they could. Cheryl had had very different ideas. She'd grown up a saver. Now she would splurge what little she had on clouds of white satin for the dress she'd dreamed of since she was a little girl.

'My people have been busy organising our civil ceremony, right down to the final details. A few forms, half an hour or so of our time—'

Cheryl's face fell. 'Oh, I was so looking forward to a church wedding. I've always wanted to walk down the aisle.'

Marco was amazed. 'A quiet wedding will mean so much more than a flashy, crowd-pleasing event.'

'I suppose so.' She sighed, knowing in her heart that it wouldn't be the sort of marriage that her dreams were made of.

Marco laughed and squeezed her hand, but there was concern in his eyes.

'It will be so much easier to have a discreet ceremony with the minimum of witnesses. Each extra person involved makes a media event more likely. I don't want my vows recorded by the world's press,' he finished darkly.

A trickle of ice ran down Cheryl's spine. Perhaps Marco wasn't so perfect after all. Not only was he trying to rush this marriage through like any other business deal, he was making sure hardly anyone knew about it.

*That will make it easier to deny in the future*, a warning voice told her.

'Wouldn't a builder from the wrong side of town like you be grateful for the advertising?' she said, but her heart wasn't in the teasing.

'Don't worry. I'll take full advantage of our arrangement. There's only one thing…' His thumb made small circles on the back of her hand. He looked troubled. 'It means inviting the press here for the first time ever—for me to show off my bride. How will you cope with all the publicity?'

'I'll manage,' Cheryl said firmly, as much to reassure herself as to convince him.

Marco lay awake for a long time that night. He had already begun to regret his hasty proposal. He'd been carried away by mistaken ideas about Cheryl. Women usually wanted him for his money, nothing more. He'd imagined Cheryl was genuinely interested in him as a man. But briefly today he had glimpsed a different side to her. Her face lit up whenever he mentioned marriage. She wanted to ditch his idea of a discreet, businesslike ceremony in favour of a full bells-and-whistles approach.

It wasn't the financial details that worried him. Cheryl's horrible past meant she was overdue some pampering. That was why he had arranged those beauty sessions for her, and their surprise lunch. She had certainly enjoyed all that. Over their meal she'd opened up, revealing herself to be an intelligent, thoughtful companion. They shared the same views on lots of topics. Taken all round, Cheryl was ideal. She was the perfect mother for Vettor, good company, good in bed, and very easy on the eyes.

But the fact she wanted him to lash out on a lavish fantasy wedding concerned him. Was this the beginning of the end? He thought back over the short time they'd spent together. Unlike his other women, Cheryl never rolled her eyes because he preferred a full English breakfast to an executive's croissant and coffee. She had remembered him picking up that splinter when he'd hardly noticed it. Though he always denied he missed hard labour, Cheryl saw through him and sensed the truth. And, best of all, her face really came alive when she was with Vettor.

Taking all those things together, Cheryl really was the employee from heaven.

Why the hell did he want to ruin things by marrying her?

# CHAPTER ELEVEN

MINUTES after Marco had finally drifted off to sleep, he was bounced awake in a flurry of noise.

'Can I come? Can I come?'

Vettor's voice rang through his head more vividly than any alarm.

'Where?' Marco hauled himself up on one elbow. He dragged one hand down over his face. It didn't make the dawn any brighter.

'When you and Cheryl get married, Uncle Marco! I want a big, big party.'

'No.'

Marco sat up abruptly, wide awake. He silenced Vettor before the little boy could get into his stride.

'When Cheryl and I get married, it's going to be a quiet wedding, with the smallest number of people we can get away with.' Marco dropped his hand heavily onto the bed, glowering at Cheryl. 'I've had barely any sleep. And I didn't ever expect to see *you* back in uniform again.'

'At the moment I'm still working under contract.'

Horrified at his reaction, Cheryl hid her feelings and bit her tongue. Like a true professional, she waited for his next instruction. Marco's attitude had changed. It sent a chill right through her. Yesterday he had made her feel special. Now his scowl drained their situation of every last drop of romance. She'd been awake half the night, getting more and more excited about becoming Marco's wife. Her excitement had reached such a pitch that she'd let Vettor into their secret almost straight away. Now the little boy knew almost as much as she did. But this morning there was a new truth written all over Marco's expression. Cheryl could see her future husband was having second thoughts. She was scared.

'Vettor, I think we'd better leave Uncle Marco to wake up in his own time,' she said diplomatically, grasping the little boy's hand. Guiding him off the bed and towards the door, she carefully avoided catching Marco's eye. But he hadn't finished with them.

'Come back here, *bimbo*.'

Leaning forward, he reached out to Vettor. The little boy sprang back at him, and was caught up in a laughing bear hug.

'OK, so I don't think our marriage is a time for wild celebration. But I can't bear to see you looking so disappointed, little one. I'll make sure you don't miss out. I'll make the party come to you—like the shops came here for Cheryl. We'll invite everybody, to satisfy their curiosity. Then maybe they'll give us some peace for the more important business of our wedding. I'll bring a whole carnival to Orchid Isle, Vettor. Just for you.'

Marco rough-housed him into another hug. He shot Cheryl a sharp look over the little boy's head as he did so.

'Settle Vettor with someone, and then come back here. We have things to arrange.'

Cheryl nodded, but said nothing. He had misunderstood her before. She had been quite happy with Marco's idea of a small, quiet wedding. She just didn't want to be robbed of the chance to dress up and enjoy herself. Yet now he was talking about entertaining on a massive scale. She'd always known marriage to him wouldn't mean being loved, nor being a cherished part of his life. Despite that, it looked as though she was going to be on his arm, in front of the world's media, playing the perfect hostess. Of all the pain he could inflict on her, that would be the worst.

The thought of socialising with all his grand friends settled on her like a lead weight. All she wanted was to be with Marco and look after Vettor. But the man who meant more to her than her own life came with a frightening social life. Knowing that was part of the deal made her feel sick with nerves.

Ten minutes later, Vettor was happily eating his breakfast beneath the vines. Cheryl couldn't delay her meeting with Marco any longer. Taut with dread, she took the walk of terror to his apartment and knocked at the door.

His voice thundered out from somewhere inside. *'Chi è là?'*

Her heart granulated. Who else *could* it be, when he had told her to come straight back? Then she remembered the stream of PAs, drivers, aides and minions who constantly invaded his life. She was only one in a long line of people clamouring for his attention.

'It's me—Cheryl,' she added, so there could be no mistake.

He threw open the door, making her jump. He was dressed in nothing but a pair of jeans, his naked brown torso rippling with strength. It was thrown into stark relief by the soft white foam of shaving soap on his face.

'You're busy, Marco. I'll come back—'

'No, come in. I'll do this later. Electric razors never do a good enough job for me.' He walked off into a side room, leaving her to enter. As she closed the main door, she heard him splashing water. Seconds later he was back, dabbing his face with a towel.

'You told me to come back.'

'Always the perfect employee,' he said, half to himself. 'Would you like some juice?'

Cheryl shook her head. A metre-wide plasma screen and a bank of sophisticated speakers formed an island in the middle of his reception area. From a fridge concealed in this entertainment centre he poured himself a glass of mineral water. After taking a token sip, he came straight to the point.

'I decided last night that I'd made a mistake— marriage to you is not such a good idea, Cheryl. But then Vettor bounced in. He obviously likes the idea of having you as stepmother.'

*It's typical of Marco to state facts without trying to cushion them*, she thought sadly. *So this won't be painless, but at least it will be quick.*

'I'm sorry, Marco. I wouldn't have told him, but…it slipped out by accident. I couldn't keep it to myself,' she said sadly. Marrying Marco would have been a sham, but at least she could have pretended he was hers. To Cheryl, he was irreplaceable. Losing him now would mean denying herself any shred of pleasure for ever.

'Things have gone further than either of us would have liked…'

*Not me*, Cheryl thought, but he hadn't finished.

'…but marriage still holds a lot of advantages, so long as neither of us is under any illusions. My legal team will have everything sewn up. When—*if*—the worst happens, you'll get a more than generous settlement. But you should know that no lawyer in the world will make any more money out of me than I'm prepared to give.'

Cheryl gaped at him in horrified surprise. She had expected him to make a speech about not wanting to marry beneath him. Instead, all he was interested in was the money side of things! It upset her so much she couldn't contain her anger.

'Well, of all the nerve! And to think I was willing to give you the benefit of the doubt when people said that money was all that mattered to you! Is that all marriage means to you, Marco? A cash settlement?'

'Of course not.' He recoiled. 'But the minute I mentioned the idea you started spending millions on white lace, carriages and a cast of thousands.'

'I don't have millions to spend,' she flared.

'Yes, but *I* do.' He bounced her own anger straight back at her.

'This isn't about *your* money. It's about *my* dreams!' Cheryl flung her arms wide with frustration. 'It's old-fashioned, but I always imagined I'd exchange vows while wearing a beautiful dress, standing hand in hand with my ideal man, in front of a priest. That idea kept me hiding my money away when my parents would have spent it all. I wanted one special day, after spending a lifetime watching other people having fun. That's all! I'd rather spend my few thousand pounds of savings on a wedding that would really mean something to both of us, for ever, than all your billions on a sham!'

Panting like a hawk, Cheryl glared at him. Marco stared straight back. It occurred to her that his expression was changing, but she didn't care. *I'm red and I'm hot and I'm furious*, Cheryl thought, *and if he doesn't like it, then that's tough!*

'How *dare* you suggest I'm doing this for dollars?' she started again. 'I'm not going to let you accuse me of being in a hurry to grab your money! Why should I be in a rush for something so meaningless when I've waited for love all my life?'

There was a moment of perfect silence. Then Marco moved forward, closing the gap between them like a trap.

Cheryl stood her ground. A few days ago she would have flinched or backed away. Now she looked up at him defiantly.

That was when she saw his face really had changed.

'Have the wedding you want,' he allowed. 'Pay for it yourself. I don't mind. All I need is a mother for Vettor. Our marriage will secure your future, and his, in the easiest way. That's all I care about.'

Cheryl blinked at him. All her rage and disappointment drained away. Was that all it took to make the great Marco Rossi understand? A bit of plain speaking?

The shock was so great, only the wistful look in his eyes stopped her being completely speechless.

'But—but what about *you*, Marco?'

'Oh…I'll get by.' He shrugged.

Something about his careless gesture spoke louder than words to Cheryl. For the first time that day a strange calmness began to steal over her. 'When it comes to life, getting by isn't enough,' she said quietly.

Their eyes met. Cheryl's body had longed for him from that first drama in the Villa Monteolio's entrance hall. Now she had tasted the delights of him, and she could not get enough. Being united beneath the stars had been wonderful beyond her wildest dreams. Coming together again in the sunlit glade had built upon that triumph. There was only one thing missing. She wanted so badly to be loved by Marco, but that didn't feature in his business plan. What could be more heavenly than to be adored by this irresistible man, to lie in his arms for ever? And yet there would always be something missing. His heart. Cheryl needed to reach out and comfort him, but his expression told her sympathy was the last thing he wanted.

She hesitated, and it was a second too long.

'I'm fine.' He broke the moment nonchalantly. 'And don't forget it's the ceremony that matters—the legal binding together of my family unit.'

His possessive words hammered her castle of dreams apart.

He couldn't love her. *He can't love anything*, Cheryl reminded herself. He scares his staff and dictates that Vettor will have a happy childhood, though he has no idea what that might mean.

'And remember—we've already had our wedding night. So you don't need to worry about me,' he added quietly.

'I'm not so sure about that.' Cheryl spoke from the shrapnel of her fantasies.

A mirthless smile lifted the corners of his lips. 'I've told you, *tesoro*, there's no need to be nervous. Not when I'm here.'

His voice was like smoke, weaving around her. The way he presented himself to her, the easy seduction of his smile, persuaded her she must be wrong. Marco had sympathised with her, comforted her and made love to her as though she was the only woman in the world. What did it matter if she was only one of dozens? The ultimate temptation of being alone with Marco in the suite that would now be theirs silenced all her misgivings. He was the one and only man for her. She had known it all along. He knew it, too.

Cheryl closed her eyes. If she didn't want to make love with him again—no, *have sex*, she corrected herself, because that was all it would be as far as Marco was concerned—she should make some excuse and walk out right now.

But Marco was already investigating the tiny buttons at the neckline of her dress. His long, sensitive fingers brushed her skin with all the delicacy of butterflies' wings. And in a rush of realisation Cheryl knew she didn't want him to stop.

He loosened her dress. She moved to let it fall free from her body. The prim cotton uniform slithered down to her ankles, revealing the delicate lace of her new underwear. Marco's hands went to her hair, releasing the pins that kept it neat. As the chestnut waves flowed free over her naked shoulders, he smiled.

'Like Venus,' he whispered with satisfaction.

His gaze evaporated every last fear lurking in Cheryl's mind. Now she knew what it was like to have someone look longingly at her, she couldn't get enough of the sensation. She gazed back at him, and then blinked. For a split second she fancied she saw something hiding deep in Marco's expression. Was that a flicker of affection deep in his clear blue eyes? She looked again. The expression was gone, but it hardly mattered. The slow tease of arousal was already misting her judgement.

'It seems a lifetime since we last made love, Cheryl.'

She was about to jump on his use of the word, but he stopped her. Pressing one long finger to her lips, he shook his head with a smile.

'Shh. I've already told you—forget everything but me.'

His voice was low with meaning. Cheryl shimmered in a haze of sensations. Her body cried out for him. Her mind reached for the satisfaction only Marco could give her. But still a web of memories trapped her imagination.

'If ours is to be such a sham of a marriage, I—I don't really want to do this again…' she whispered.

They both knew it was a lie. Her dark eyes begged him to take the lead. Although motionless, she reached out to Marco.

He stared into her eyes for a long, long time.

'Fine,' he murmured at last. 'If you want to call a halt, I'll finish my shave. You can go and practice changing from Nanny into Mamma. I won't distract you any more.'

He made to move away, to take his hands from her. She stopped him.

'I'm yours, Marco.' Her voice was soft, but urgent. 'We both know it. Take me…'

Marco silenced her with a kiss that swept every one of her doubts away.

For now.

# CHAPTER TWELVE

FROM then on, Cheryl's days and nights were filled with Marco. His passion was as relentless as the sea, and she couldn't get enough of him. Her life passed in a delicious warm haze of desire. Only one shadow darkened her horizon. The Party. She tried hard to stifle her fears, blocking them by concentrating on Marco instead. That wasn't difficult. His body was totally hers. He caressed her and seduced her to heights of pleasure she had never known before. Marco and Cheryl's nights were spent in passion, not sleep.

Vettor had picked up on the magic shimmering between them. From being a good child, he'd turned into an ideal one. Tempted by fresh fish from the ocean and all kinds of tropical fruits, he ate and ate. When Cheryl could bear to tear her attention away from Marco, she saw Vettor filling out and ripening in the endless sun.

'I wish we could stay here for ever,' she said dreamily some weeks later, as Marco rocked them both in the hammock.

He clicked his tongue. 'It can't be done, I'm afraid. There's only so much work I can do on a laptop. After the party this evening I must get back to the office. It keeps my workforce up to speed.'

Any mention of the party made Cheryl's blood run cold. She lifted her head from his chest to look round at him, trying to reassure herself.

'But you'll be spending plenty of time with me? Just the two of us? On our own?'

His arm tightened around her and he kissed the crown of her head.

'Of course. I'll make sure of it.'

No sooner had Marco made that promise, than he broke it. A noisy fleet of helicopters roared in overhead, and he sat up.

'I must go. Our party arrives in boxes, and they're all aboard those choppers. Let's start getting ready. Our guests will soon be arriving.'

Your *guests*, Cheryl thought with dread.

Vettor had no worries at all. With a whoop of joy, he forgot the glittering beetle he had been watching and charged off towards the apartments.

'I'll be right in to help you,' Marco called after him.

Cheryl was half out of the hammock, but when she heard him say that she stopped. 'That's my job. What about me?'

His eyes still on Vettor, Marco reached for her hand. She made it easy for him by catching hold, but his intention was not helping her to her feet. Instead, he gave her a cheerful squeeze and let go straight away.

'Surely you don't need to do anything? You're beautiful enough already, *cara*.'

Throwing her a quick smile, he abandoned her for the complex and Vettor. Cheryl's plan to bring them together had worked brilliantly for the little boy. But not for her. *If only Marco realised how I felt*, she thought sadly as she followed them. *I'm a spare part today. I'm no longer needed as a nanny, and Marco's staff do absolutely everything else for us.*

The only thing left for her was to act as hostess at his party. And she was dreading it more than a trip to the dentist. The guest list ran to several pages of closely typed paper. When she looked down the names she didn't recognise any apart from ones she had seen in newspapers.

Marco had brushed aside her worries with his usual ease.

'If we invite everyone, that'll satisfy their curiosity. It will save inviting them back to the Villa Monteolio after the event. The press will get their pictures, and won't need to gatecrash our big day. We'll give everyone the best of everything. They'll be dazzled by our generosity and your beauty.'

Cheryl had not been convinced. 'I wish I didn't have to attend. I might as well not be there anyway—I'll just fade into the background. You handle people so much better than I do.'

'You'll manage—you'll learn.' Marco's belief in her was total. 'It's a case of having to do it. And there will be an English couple here, so you'll have something in common with them at least.'

'The Duke and Duchess of Compton?' Cheryl squeaked. 'What makes you think I'll be able to talk to them?'

'Oh, you'll be fine. I knew Sophie when she was nothing but a girl on the party circuit. If she tries anything, just tell her *you're* the one I'm marrying,' Marco said airily. 'If that doesn't work, remind her who bought her husband out of a very deep hole last year.'

That hadn't reassured Cheryl one bit. The Duchess of Compton was a famous beauty, and rumoured to have a lot of lovers. What if she set her sights on Marco?

Worse was to come. Cheryl had thought her spirits couldn't sink any lower, but as the guests began jetting in to Orchid Isle she found out how wrong she could be.

None of the women reached double figures in their dress sizes. They were all as thin as sticks of celery, and as they descended from their private planes, their angular faces turned this way and that. At first Cheryl thought they were admiring Orchid Isle. The multiple explosions of paparazzi flash guns soon put that idea out of her head. They were posing. Image was the only thing anyone was interested in.

But Orchid Isle lived up to all their guests' expectations. Cheryl was relieved to hear nothing but coos and compliments. And despite all the famous people thronging his island, Marco was the star. Everyone wanted to be photographed with him.

'Just one more, *tesoro*.' He took Cheryl's hands and persuaded her into position beside him again. 'I know how much you hate it, but if I show you off on this occasion you'll never need to pose for them again.'

Reluctantly, Cheryl agreed. She fitted so neatly beneath Marco's arm it felt like the most natural place in the world for her. And at least she had the comfort of him as she smiled for the cameras yet again. She wished she could fall into a pose as naturally as Sophie, the Duke of Compton's wife, did. Cheryl could see that camera lenses and lovers alike adored the woman.

It made her look at Marco more carefully than ever. She noticed his behaviour changed whenever the dashing duchess came near. His smile was always devastating, but then it developed a new intensity. He seemed to consciously turn his back on Sophie so he could speak to Cheryl. It was lovely to have his full attention as he brushed a windblown curl from her face or a petal from her dress, but it was making Cheryl feel uneasy. Was Marco trying to hide something?

Her insecurity grew when he suggested they split up and circulate among their guests. Before she could protest, he disappeared into the throng with Vettor.

Cheryl surveyed the mass of people, wondering what to do. Waiters in dazzling white jackets and black ties brought around a constant supply of canapés and drinks. She took a nibble from one, and a glass from another. Instantly she felt better. Having something in her hands helped take her mind off her fears. The champagne was flowing freely, and there were all sorts of delicacies to choose from. The arrangements of smoked salmon, caviar and truffles set on silver salvers were works of art.

Everything looked so pretty it was almost a shame to spoil the displays. That didn't worry the male guests, who ate everything they were offered and were quick to ask for more, but their wives and other arm candy were more particular. Cheryl never saw any of them eat anything. Looks were exchanged whenever a waiter offered them a canapé, though champagne was apparently allowed on the latest celebrity diet. She, too, tried to resist, and when Marco's retained photographer started exhibiting portraits of the guests on a giant screen she needed something to cheer her up.

She hardly recognised her own image. Projected twenty feet above the crowd, in the new black and white silk dress Marco had chosen for her, she looked both stunning and serene. In reality, she felt like a zebra in a herd of gazelles. She was totally out of place, and had never felt more at risk. None of the men could take their eyes off her cleavage. None of the females could take their eyes off Marco. But at least the women were being nice to her—or so she thought.

When all the noise and crowding became too much, Cheryl dived into the vast marquee that had been set up as a ladies' restroom. There she cowered in one of its silk-draped cubicles. She knew she couldn't stay there for ever, but just as she was screwing up the courage to face everyone again, a racket of heels and squeals erupted outside. Jumping back into her haven, she pulled the pink curtains closed. She tried to tell herself it was because the cubicle's arrangement of lilies and roses needed attention. It didn't. The real reason was Sophie Compton. Cheryl had recognised her voice, and couldn't face her figure.

'Of course this Cheryl Lane is a total *nobody*!' The duchess's cultured tones rang through the whole structure as a group of women clattered into the marquee behind her. 'God knows where Marco found her. As I told him, you can always stoop and pick up nothing.'

Cheryl burned with indignation. She had guessed it would be bad. Now she knew.

'So she hasn't got a title?' another voice enquired.

'Good God, no!'

'Well, she's definitely *not* one of us!'

That was the transatlantic drawl of a famous TV anchorwoman. Now Cheryl knew her shame would be broadcast coast to coast.

'Have you *seen* the amount she eats?'

That remark was greeted by a tinkling riot of laughter. Inside the cubicle, Cheryl's shame turned to awful, crawling despair.

A fourth voice chimed in. 'She's stuffing in the canapés—I saw her.'

This sparked more laughter all round, and then, fuelled by their gossip, the hunting party snapped shut their compacts and quickly moved out of the marquee.

Cheryl buried her face in the curtains, gripping the pink silk until it creased beyond rescue. She dared not cry. Unlike her tormentors, she had no idea how to repair the make-up mask her personal beautician had so carefully applied. All she could do was hide, racked by painful dry sobs.

Was this what her life would be like from now on? People saying one thing to her face, another behind her back? While Marco sailed on a tide of admiration, sharks surrounded her. All her life she had felt as though she was on the outside, looking in. Now she was wallowing in the thick of things. Once she had dreamed of being the centre of attention. Living it was going to be a nightmare. She loved Marco so much it hurt. Yet why should he ever love *her*? He only needed her because it suited him to have the best possible mother for Vettor. How would she cope, knowing that he might find satisfaction in her arms, but never love? That wasn't life. It was a life sentence.

She cowered in her cubicle until she heard the click of more heels on the smooth veneered floor of the restroom. The fear of hearing herself talked about again catapulted her out of her refuge. She was sure she must have made lots of mistakes, but at least people would smile to her face. They wouldn't dare say anything nasty to her in public.

Would they?

Despite the cavalcade of entertainers and musicians, sumptuous catering and a final display of fireworks, Cheryl couldn't enjoy anything. By the time their final guests were preparing to leave, dawn was shimmering across the ocean. Marco slipped his arm around her waist as they walked along the shore together. Flower petals blown out to sea from the party danced around their feet, brought back by mischievous wavelets.

'Thank you, Cheryl. I know how difficult it must have been for you, among all those people. If it's any consolation, I prefer it when it's just the two of us.' He gave her a squeeze, and held her close as they strolled on.

His silence was contented. Cheryl's was full of doubt. *Which two does he mean? Me, the greedy nobody? Or Sophie Compton, elegant duchess?*

'Did you enjoy the party, Cheryl?'

'Oh, yes,' she replied quietly.

'Are you happy?' he murmured.

'Very.'

'Good.'

His voice oozed satisfaction. Cheryl was glad—although neither of her answers could have been further from the truth.

They wandered towards the helipad, watching the remains of the party being packed away in ice. Everything was being transported back to the Villa Monteolio so that the staff there could enjoy Marco's generosity.

'Why don't I go and arrange a very special breakfast for us? We could have it served in bed...' He nuzzled into her ear.

Cheryl turned to him. Before she could speak, he kissed her. The passion between them sparked, but Cheryl knew it was nothing without love.

*But this isn't how it should be*, she thought. *We're about to get married!*

And that was the terrible thing. It would never be a real marriage of the sort she so desperately wanted. She needed to be enclosed, enfolded and included for the first time in her life. Marco could certainly provide all that—when he wanted sex. But his lifestyle wasn't something she wanted to be a part of. All she wanted was this gorgeous man walking along beside her—but apparently he came as part of a horrible celebrity package. The party had been a taste of things to come—all show, but no substance. Nothing was real any more. The heart-stopping moments she had shared with Marco were a dim and distant memory, receding as though she was looking at them down the wrong end of a telescope.

Marco left her, heading for the apartment complex. Behind her, the last boxes were loaded, and the helicopter blades began to turn.

Almost as if acting on instinct and self-preservation, Cheryl turned her back on Orchid Isle and jumped onto the departing aircraft.

Marco smiled as he strolled towards the complex. His heart felt lighter than it had done in years. He no longer felt the need to submerge himself in work. His obsession with it had been an attempt to prove memories had no power over him. Cheryl had changed all that. She was transforming his life. He saw things so much more clearly now. By encouraging him to spend time with Vettor, she was improving all their lives. *Especially mine*, he thought.

Then the giant screen above the dance floor caught his eye. It showed three men, all immaculate in designer tuxedos, each with a champagne glass in their soft, pale hands. One was an international playboy, and the second was a gambler, famous for beating the house in Monte Carlo. It took Marco slightly longer to recognise the third. When he did, he swore softly.

'*Mio Dio*, that's *me*!' he said aloud.

There was no one to hear him except a chorus of parakeets in the surrounding trees. He thought back to the conversation going on when the photographer had taken that snap. The other two men had been trying to outdo each other, listing their latest extravagances. Marco was openly proud of his self-made millions, but their preening left him cold. He had smiled with them, but only because he was a polite host.

An old saying crossed his mind. *You can tell the quality of a man by the company he keeps.*

*Why am I wasting my time on people like that?* he

thought. Suddenly, all he wanted was Cheryl—now and for ever.

Realising that made him laugh out loud. Above him, the parakeets spun out from the treetops like streamers, and he smiled up at the sky as they flew by.

Cheryl had no idea where she would go or what she would do. All she knew was that she had to get away from Orchid Isle.

*I can't stay here a minute longer*, she told herself. *I'm not me any more! All those beauticians and personal dressers, and what's it all for? Marco didn't fall in love with my appearance. He didn't fall in love with me at all. He's marrying me for what I can do for him. All this pointless extravagance is making me a laughing stock in front of his friends. He's better off without all that. I can't spend my time trying to live up to the expectations of other people. It's like being a child all over again, and I can't cope with it.*

She couldn't bear to think how Vettor would react when he was told there would be no wedding. She stared out of the helicopter window, blind to the beauty beyond. All she could see was a future filled with disasters, mistakes, blunders and social gaffes. *Mum was right. I should never have tried to get on in life*, Cheryl thought.

She wasn't suited for high society. The only thing she would get from marrying her boss was a lot of people talking behind her back.

Marco could do without her. He'd never needed her physically, in the heart-stopping, emotional way she needed him. He had Vettor to absorb all his love now.

They were devoted to each other. It wasn't as though Cheryl could do anything for them in a professional role either. She'd been employed as a nanny when Vettor had no one. Now the little boy had Marco's full attention. How could he ever be expected to think of a humble ex-member of staff as his mother?

While talking to the chef about breakfast, Marco spotted some of his staff draping fresh figs with prosciutto. The kitchens were so well organised they were already getting ready for lunch. Knowing how much Cheryl loved the fruit, he took a few. Dropping them in a basket, he headed off to find her. After a few seconds, a sudden thought struck him. It gave him such a surprise he stopped dead. He'd partied all night, he'd just thrown his chef into confusion, and now he was taking time off for an impromptu meal when he should have been working.

He couldn't imagine doing this for anyone but Cheryl. Looking down at the violet-dark figs he was carrying, he rubbed his chin, considering. Now he came to think of it, life had changed for him in a lot of little ways lately. And the improvement had accelerated under the azure skies of Orchid Isle the moment he took Cheryl into his bed. *She's got a lot to answer for*, he told himself with a lazy smile.

When he got to the airstrip, he found it deserted. Wandering back to the complex, he was disturbed to find no sign of her anywhere. Vettor was still sound asleep, but where was Cheryl? If he didn't find her soon he'd have no excuse for skipping a meeting with his attorney. He smiled. This new and improved Cheryl could make him forget everything else on the planet. She made him resent every second he spent away from her. His lawyers were complaining he hadn't signed the pre-nup agreement yet. He would never have forgotten that lifestyle-saving detail with any other woman.

*You've got a lot to answer for, Miss Lane-soon-to-be-Signora-Rossi!* He said to himself as he set off on a circuit of the island in search of her. Then he stopped again. *Signora Rossi…* It sounded almost as good as she did. He grinned. The more he thought about Cheryl, the wider his smile became…

Right until the moment one of the airfield staff told him she'd left Orchid Isle on the last helicopter.

Marco could hardly believe his bird of paradise had flown. He dashed back to their apartment. There was no note, but there couldn't be any doubt about it. He tried to think back over their last conversation, their last lovemaking…it was hopeless. His brain had stopped functioning. He couldn't make sense of anything.

Reaching the heart of their suite, he stopped at the foot of the bed. Housekeeping had not visited their apartment since their last passionate lovemaking, but the duvet was folded back neatly, as Cheryl always left it. The bolsters still bore the slight impressions they had left. *Last passionate lovemaking?* He brought himself up short. The words had an unlucky finality about them, but Marco Rossi had never lost a woman yet—and he didn't intend to start now.

He grabbed the bedside phone to mobilise every member of his staff, all over the globe. He'd send them all out to track Cheryl down, to bring her back.

He'd spend all the money it took to retrieve her, to find out why—

Then he paused, and thought back to his sister Rosalia. When he had discovered his money had been paying for her drug habit, he'd thrown more and more of it at her problem. He'd funded Rosalia and her boyfriend through rehab, and arranged for them to stay at the world's most exclusive spa to try to encourage them further.

Marco had been due to take them there, but he'd hung on at the office that day, to clinch one last deal. Instead of running them to the airport himself, he'd delegated the task to one of his drivers. The man had been a new recruit, untried and untested. Desperate to impress, he'd taken one too many risks on the twisting road and killed himself and his passengers.

To Marco's way of thinking, if you had a coin, you had a friend. Yet his desperate need to create security for himself had killed Vettor's parents. *His* work ethic had helped bring about their problems. Later, it had made him entrust them to a crazy driver. His wealth had created their tragedy, and it hadn't been able to solve it.

Whatever had made Cheryl run away, Marco realised he couldn't fix things by simply casting his net of gold. The only thing he wanted was Cheryl. And he wanted her badly enough to show her by his own actions. Not by sending someone else to find her.

Without realising it, Marco had moved around to Cheryl's side of the bed. Leaning over, he brushed her pillow and inhaled. A last, lingering memory of her perfume crept into the deepest corners of his soul. *She's brought me so many pleasures*, Marco thought with a rush of adrenaline.

Losing sight of the really important things in life meant he had been too absorbed to keep his sister Rosalia safe. No way was he going to make the same mistake with Cheryl!

He had to find out where she was, and why. And he was going to do it right now.

The helicopter landed on Marco's luxury liner. Cheryl got out, knowing she should go below without looking back at the distant pleasures of Orchid Isle. That was what common sense told her—but Marco Rossi was the enemy of common sense. He had totally bewitched her.

She went to the rail, twisting her handkerchief into a hangman's noose. How could she sacrifice all those perfect days and nights with him? The feel of his warm smooth skin gliding against hers? Velvet nights of ecstasy and dawns filled with passion? The only reason she could do it was because he had given her everything except the only thing she wanted from him—his love.

*I must be mad*, she thought.

Cheryl might not have much experience of the world, but she knew one thing for certain. No other man would ever mean anything to her again. All she wanted was Marco. She tried to block out the past few weeks so her mind couldn't dwell on the big, empty space where her heart had been. It didn't work. She was desolate.

Squeezing her eyes tightly shut, she tried to make her mind a blank. Her senses rebelled. She even started hearing things. Above the small sounds of shipboard life going on around her, she heard the rasp of a speedboat. She tried to tell herself not to be silly, but it got

closer. Suddenly everyone around her was galvanised
into action. Excited shouts and the racket of running
feet opened her eyes to a surprise arrival.

Marco was swinging the Orchid Isle speedboat
alongside his liner in a flurry of spray. Abandoning it to
leap onto the steps leading up to the deck, he took them
three at a time. He was at the top before anyone could
open the rail for him. He burst through it, eyes blazing.

'Cheryl?'

His expression was grim, but he spoke her name
with such soft sibilance her heart nearly stopped. In that
instant time stood still. Cheryl shut her eyes again,
knowing her own desperate need for Marco could never
make up for the gulf that separated them.

'I'm sorry, Marco. I just can't do this.'

There was another rattle of hurrying feet, and then
silence.

'What? *What* can't you do?'

'All this.'

She opened her eyes again to gaze at him, unable to
keep the misery from her voice. He had dismissed all
his staff. Finding herself alone with him, Cheryl waved
her hands in a hopeless gesture of misery.

'I don't fit in here. If I marry you, I won't be a
member of your staff any more. But that doesn't mean
I can hope to be part of your world. Your party proved
that to me once and for all.'

Marco stepped forward. Taking hold of her wrists,
he squeezed them gently.

'Then forget it. Let me take you home.'

Stunned, she stared at him. In her confusion she
could put only one meaning on his words.

'To England?'

Marco's beautiful blue gaze was hooded as he shook his head slowly. 'No. I mean *our* home, *tesoro*. The Villa Monteolio.'

Cheryl's head drooped. It was her turn to shake her head as she stared down at the deck. As he watched, a single tear fell onto their entwined hands.

'There's no point, Marco! I don't fit into your world. You said you wanted a mother for Vettor. But that time has passed. You don't need one now. Anyone can see you're the best and only parent he needs.' Her mind flew back to them playing in the surf on Orchid Isle. 'When you're together, it's the two of you against the world. You're going to conquer it together. I used to think I'd have to be the one who was always there for Vettor. But he doesn't need me any more.'

'Yes, he does. And so do I, Cheryl. For a long time I lost sight of the only truly important thing in life. Relationships are the only things that matter. And to me, right here and now, that means only one person. *You.*'

His voice throbbed with intent, and his eyes were burning.

'I want you, Cheryl. None of this means anything to me—not this vessel, nor the party, our guests, or even Orchid Isle. I'd give it all up in an instant for you, *mio tesoro*. You found my heart. When you left the island just now, I discovered you'd taken my soul with you.'

Their eyes met, and suddenly nothing mattered any more. They were within reach of each other again. That was enough. Cheryl lifted her hand to touch his shoulder at the exact moment he did the same thing to her. She sighed with longing, but Marco was already taking the initiative. In seconds he was kissing every thought from her mind.

Much later, when she could catch her breath, she looked up into his face with an expression of pure adoration.

'Oh, Marco, I missed you from the second I got onto that helicopter! I am so very sorry—'

He kissed her again.

'No—wait, Marco. I have to apologise—'

He wasn't listening. He was too busy celebrating her body. All he wanted was to hold her in his arms. After a paradise of kisses, he finally leaned back a little way and gazed down at her.

'I don't want your apologies, my love. Getting you back was all I ever needed. Every second we were apart was torture for me. I thought I'd lost you for ever,' he murmured tenderly.

He was looking at her in such a way…Cheryl knew she had to tell him everything.

'It started yesterday, at the party. You arranged it, all your friends were there, and you couldn't keep your eyes off the Duchess of Compton. The *last* thing you needed was an awkward girl like me who didn't know her place.'

'That's rubbish! I wanted to make sure Sophie kept her claws out of you, that's all. Cheryl Lane, you mean more to me than all of those people put together—men, women, megastars, the whole lot.'

His hands tightened on her shoulders. There was such fire in his brilliant blue eyes Cheryl didn't doubt him for a second. Even so, there was one horrible truth that had to be exorcised.

'I overheard somebody saying terrible things. They made me sound as though I was a dead weight around your neck.'

'Who was it?'

His voice was a dangerous growl. Cheryl felt her anger surge through him, and sensed she held Sophie Compton's future in her hands. Revenge would have been sweet, but Cheryl knew she could never forgive herself for telling tales. Marco's courage was infectious, so she came to a decision.

'I wouldn't tell you even if I knew. It's in the past, Marco. If I don't want people to say things like that about me in the future, then I've got to make more of an effort. I'll have to learn to face them with more spirit next time.'

'There isn't going to be a next time. You'll never have to face that sort again,' he stated firmly, stroking her hair. 'I had the party for Vettor's benefit, but it's the last time I will do anything like that, believe me. I knew you wouldn't enjoy the day but— *Dio!* I should have noticed the warning signs and been more understanding. And you've got plenty of spirit already. Along with all the other qualities I've been looking for all my life. You're the first person who's never wanted anything from me, Cheryl. Instead, you've shown an interest in me, and turned my lonely nephew into a cheerful little boy into the bargain.'

'You did that yourself. You're his father now.' Cheryl smiled. She couldn't decide which she loved best—the gentle way Marco was looking at her, or the unusual warmth in his voice.

'From now on I've decided to take a more relaxed view of life. Like you,' he added.

She laughed. 'You're making fun of me!'

'Not really.' He pulled her in close again, and she felt him kiss the top of her head. 'I've been too engrossed, far too passionate about my work in the past, *tesoro*.' He spoke with his chin on her hair. She felt the movement, and knew he was more comfortable speaking from his heart when he could not see her face. Cheryl relaxed. Marco didn't need her to say anything. She could tell from his silence. It was more reflective than usual.

'Come home to Italy with me now. I need you, Cheryl. So does Vettor. You've been gone for less than an hour, but from the moment he woke up he's been driving everyone mad with *"Where's Cheryl?"* How am I supposed to cope with that?'

Cheryl tried to laugh. 'He'll be missing *you* now, too,' she reassured him. 'You give him everything he needs, backed up with all the experience and common sense he needs to keep him grounded.'

'And now I've got the perfect female carer for him, too.'

Cheryl gazed up at him in wonder for a long time.

'Can I hope that means me?' she breathed softly.

'There could never be anyone else but you for me, my love.'

'Oh, Marco…' Her voice trembled into silence. All the pain of isolation poured out from somewhere Cheryl had never known existed. 'Marco, I want you to be my husband for real. And Vettor to be my little boy.'

It was the last tiny piece of her jigsaw. She hadn't known it was missing until this moment, but now it felt as vital as the final clue in a drama. She had never been loved as a child. Now she was desperate to make up for it with motherless Vettor and her gorgeous fiancé.

'Shh, my love.' He stroked her tenderly. 'We will love Vettor as if he were our own son, and he will be a brother to *our* children. Yours and mine,' he added with another kiss.

There was such feeling in his voice and touch; Cheryl was swept right back to the first time they made love. She felt him lace his fingers behind her back. With a sigh of contentment she relaxed against him.

Nestling his cheek against her hair, he spoke quietly into its warmth. 'Until I met you, Cheryl, I wondered why I bothered with life. I'd been working so hard for so long, I'd lost sight of the important things. But when I look at you it all comes flooding back. Let me make you happy. Let me keep you safe beside me at the Villa Monteolio for as long as grass grows and birds sing.'

Cheryl had dreamed of this moment from the instant they'd met. Now Marco was turning her life into something better than any fantasy. She took a moment to revel in it before saying anything.

'Is that another proposal, Marco?'

'Of course it is,' he whispered. 'Fill my life, my love, and I'll make every day perfection for you. That's guaranteed.'

'I know, Marco. You've already made all my dreams come true. So the answer to your question is…yes…' she murmured, closing her eyes in anticipation of another delicious kiss.

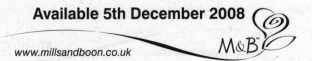

# *Celebrate 100 years of pure reading pleasure with Mills & Boon®*

To mark our centenary, each month we're publishing a special 100th Birthday Edition. These celebratory editions are packed with extra features and include a FREE bonus story.

Plus, you have the chance to enter a fabulous monthly prize draw. See 100th Birthday Edition books for details.

*Now that's worth celebrating!*

### September 2008

**Crazy about her Spanish Boss by Rebecca Winters**
Includes FREE bonus story
*Rafael's Convenient Proposal*

### November 2008

**The Rancher's Christmas Baby
by Cathy Gillen Thacker**
Includes FREE bonus story *Baby's First Christmas*

### December 2008

**One Magical Christmas by Carol Marinelli**
Includes FREE bonus story *Emergency at Bayside*

Look for Mills & Boon® 100th Birthday Editions at your favourite bookseller or visit www.millsandboon.co.uk

# 4 Books
## and a surprise gift!

We would like to take this opportunity to thank you for reading this Mills & Boon® book by offering you the chance to take FOUR more specially selected titles from the Modern™ series absolutely FREE! We're also making this offer to introduce you to the benefits of the Mills & Boon® Book Club™—

- ★ **FREE home delivery**
- ★ **FREE gifts and competitions**
- ★ **FREE monthly Newsletter**
- ★ **Exclusive Mills & Boon Book Club offers**
- ★ **Books available before they're in the shops**

Accepting these FREE books and gift places you under no obligation to buy, you may cancel at any time, even after receiving your free shipment. Simply complete your details below and return the entire page to the address below. You don't even need a stamp!

**YES!** Please send me 4 free Modern books and a surprise gift. I understand that unless you hear from me, I will receive 6 superb new titles every month for just £2.99 each, postage and packing free. I am under no obligation to purchase any books and may cancel my subscription at any time. The free books and gift will be mine to keep in any case.

P8ZEF

Ms/Mrs/Miss/Mr ......................................................Initials ..................................

Surname ................................................................................................................

Address..................................................................... **BLOCK CAPITALS PLEASE**

.............................................................................................................................

.................................................................Postcode ......................................

**Send this whole page to:**
**UK: FREEPOST CN81, Croydon, CR9 3WZ**